MW01436484

HOPE:
ALL OTHER GROUND IS SINKING SAND

Gina M. Jones

Hope: All Other Ground Is Sinking Sand is a work of fiction. Names, characters, places, and incidents are the products of the author's imagination or are used fictitiously. Any resemblance to actual events, locales, or persons, living or dead, is entirely coincidental.

Copyright © 2022 by Gina M. Jones

ISBN: 978-1-66784-747-4

All rights reserved.

Library of Congress Cataloging-in-Publication Data

No part of this publication may be reproduced, distributed, or transmitted in any form or by any means, including photocopying, recording, or other electronic or mechanical methods, without the prior written permission of the publisher, except in the care of brief quotations embodied in critical reviews and certain other noncommercial uses permitted by copyright law. For permission requests, contact include Gina M. Jones e-mail peacfo@aol.com

Editing: Kayla Witherspoon, BookBaby

First Edition

Book cover created and designed by Monica Dodson

Published in the United States

BookBaby
7905 N. Crescent Blvd.
Pennsauken, NJ 08110
info@bookbaby.com

Dedication

This book is dedicated to my father Charles Sanford Jones. He went home to be with the Lord before I completed it. One day, a year before he passed, I read a chapter to my mom and my sisters, and I thought my father was sitting in the chair, asleep. I didn't know he was listening. After reading a few of the chapters to them, I walked past my dad and he said, "You wrote that?"

I stopped in my tracks, and said, "Yes," with a big smile.

He went on to say, "I like that. You should finish writing it."

Those words from my father gave me the motivation to be all that I thought I could be.

I did it Daddy; by the Grace of God, I finished it. I know your spirit was with me every step of the way.

Daddy, you are forever my Hero.

Your "Baby Girl"

Acknowledgments

I give all the glory to my Lord and Savior Jesus Christ. He has allowed a dream of mine to come into fruition. He opened doors and made a way. He healed me and allowed me to come back and finish what I started. I am forever grateful to Him. The best is still yet to come. Thank you, Father God, for your blessings.

I want to thank my beautiful family for always loving me, praying for me, and supporting me. My praying, beautiful mother who loves me beyond measure. I also want to thank my siblings Deb, Nat, and Rodney (including my brothers in love, Ron and Mike, and sister in love, Brenda) for being my prayer partners and my rock. I thank God for you all every day. I pray I have made you proud of me along the way. Thank you all for being "the wind beneath my wings."

To Shawn, my beautiful partner/kid/BFF: thank you for your undying support, love, and encouragement, in sickness and in health. You knew my dream was to write a book, and you stuck by me and pushed me beyond my limits. When I lost my ability to speak or write, you made sure that I had everything I needed to practice writing again. You were my voice. I want to thank your family for their unconditional love and support in helping you nurse me back to health and taking care of me when I could not take care of myself. The Lord gave you the strength to do all that you did for me Shawn. You are a beautiful soul, and I will always be indebted to you. I thank God for you! In the words of Maya Angelou: "Thank you for being a part of my existence." I love you!

A special thanks to my niece Kayla for her excellent editing skills. You rock, Kayla Poo! I also want to thank my talented friend and artist Monica Dodson for creating for me undoubtedly eye-catching book cover. Thank you for bringing my book to life.

To all of my ancestors who had dreams, but could not see them through, I know you are smiling down on me for not giving up on mine.

Preface

Candace, a young colored girl raised in the south in the late 1940's, never knew what having hope felt like. She feared that people would find out that her son could not speak, so she kept a secret for as long as she could. Some children have been placed in mental hospitals for the very same thing, or worse. This was her biggest fear. As news of her son's disability travels through her hometown Jacksonville, North Carolina, Candace takes a leap of faith and decides to trust a teacher, with the hope that will change both her and her son's lives forever.

HOPE:
All Other Ground is Sinking Sand

Chapter 1

The Beginning

Each time I see the sun peeping through the darkness, I feel the stress of the day already. My mind races to answer questions I don't even know to ask yet. I'm tired. And my body tells me that every day. How come hope is never my destination? Maybe 'cause pain has been my friend. If I told them I had hope, they would laugh at me. I can't even think of a better life other than having meat for supper instead of oatmeal and crackers. I look at Dre, my baby, and smile and whisper a prayer everyday: Lord, please give me hope for his life.

His daddy was my mistake and could be the reason for the way my son is. If I ever thought I was in love, it was the moment I laid my eyes on my son, Dre. I knew, and so did God, that his daddy wasn't meant for me. After three months of courting and touchin', I still didn't know much about him. So when the news came- "Youse in that way."-I felt numb. Pregnant!

What am I gonna tell mama? Even though she would probably know as soon as she saw me. The older women have a way knowing some how. How can I tell the daddy when he has already left Jacksonville? He was in the Marines, traveling on the big ships that carried them to and from different places, and they stopped in Wilmington for a few months. This was the colored girl's dream—to find a husband and move on to a better life. It did me the opposite. He got what was easy for him and left. He will never know what we made together. I always thought his touch was something special when we made love. Well, I reckon Dre was the love we made. My heart melts every time I see my baby boy.

I guess I better gather my apron and sewing stuff and get ready for work. Work is a ten-hour day in a factory, sewing clothes for a company that's out of the country. "Mr. Harry, I have the materials cut and narrowed down with colors matchin'." I'm scared of the response, so I never look up. He is so hateful.

"It doesn't make much difference now. I have to let you go."

He wouldn't look at my face. My palms were so sweaty I just wiped them on my apron and prayed I wouldn't start crying in front of him. "Mr. Harry, I don't know what I would do without this job. I got Dre who I have to raise and we depend on the money."

"Well, I need to let somebody go and you only got one child. The rest of the gals here got three or four chillun."

The whisper of hope for Dre's life rushes through my mind. I never understood what it meant to have dignity, but I heard people talk about it as if everybody should have it. I left without him seeing a single tear. I hear Mr. Harry say as I walked out, "Hold your head high and have hope." There is that word again—hope. Seems like you must have a whole lot of money to have it.

What am I going to do now? I didn't like being in that hot warehouse anyway. I have to tell mama something. I sure can't tell her a story. She would know right away if I was telling something not true.

I don't like leaving Dre with mama on the days I worked. Dre can be too much for her sometimes. The first thing mama wants to do is beat him when he has a fit or a tantrum. If he could talk, I would know what ails him. Papa never asks questions about Dre not talking. Papa is an easy-going man with a lot of patience. People around here say that's the spirit of the Lord in him. Papa would talk to Dre as if he understands him. I believe Dre knows a safe feeling when he is around mama and papa. I know when I walk in the door, he is going to be sitting at papa's feet. That makes him feel safe I reckon. I pray that one day he will know that he is loved.

CHAPTER 2

Facing the Hard Question

My neighbor, May Esther, popped over, and we sat on the porch to talk, dreamed, and laughed while she drank a beer and I sipped on lemonade.

"I tell you, that boy got more energy than a Greyhound. How in the world you get him to sleep?" she says.

I laughed. "Shoot! Most days I sit out here and let him chase anything moving in the yard."

"Have you ever thought of putting him in a school so they can teach him to talk or say words?"

I gave her a look 'cause I never thought she paid Dre any mind. He never said a word to her or me. Ever since I realized Dre wouldn't talk, I kept it to myself, but folk so nosey and don't mind their own life. I got so used to the sounds he would make I never thought of teaching him words. Now that he is four, I was scared and embarrassed to tell anybody. I worried about people trying to take him from me and put him in the state hospital thinking he was retarded or an idiot. I know people would call me a bad mama.

I ignored May Esther, avoiding eye contact. "I figure if I pray hard enough, it will happen. He will talk."

"Yeah, I hear you with your faith and all, Candace. But what people don't realize is that God gives us ways to get things done. The schoolhouse on Jackie Road got them teachers up there to teach kids how to read and write, so I know they can teach how to talk."

I was so confused, I was afraid to ask questions. May Esther never seemed like a gossiper, but I didn't want to take chances. "Come on, Dre; let's go in the house, Shug." I loved seeing him with so much energy.

"Candace, I didn't mean to make you uncomfortable. I love you and Dre so much, you're family to me."

May Esther grabbed her beer and walked off the porch and patted Dre on his head. She saw I had nothing to say, but I didn't know how to answer her question of him being in school. I couldn't recall ever having to think these thoughts about school. I wouldn't allow myself to think about it. I knew it was a selfish thing to not ask for help. What if they say I'm not fit to raise him? I had seen it happen here in the south. I couldn't let that happen. "Lord, God, please send an angel," I say it like Ms. Agnes, the white lady me and mama used to work for. I pray, "Please send an angel."

Chapter 3

May Esther

I always liked talking to May Esther. She was the school I never went to. I would sit and listen to her talk about life as if she was reading a book out loud to me. The words would come out like she was singing. I sometimes wondered how she dealt with a man who was never around, and bossed her into a creating a nightlife in her own home. I saw the men going in and out of there, but it wasn't my business. I didn't say a word.

"I have to get ready," May Esther said to herself, looking in the mirror. "My first job will be here in a minute banging on the door like a fool. It's a shame I have so much love for someone else, but he doesn't care for me and I want."

"May! May Esther!! Where you at? It's almost noon and you layin' round here like you don't have nothing to do."

" Nicky, I'm tired and that last bastard left so late last night," she replied.

May Esther's boyfriend Nicky never hit her, but he'd bruised her soul without a lick.

"I told you, May; it will get easier in a few weeks, but right now we need the money."

"Nicky, I'm tired. And you say the same thing to me all the time. It ain't you givin' yourself away." Saying so, May turned her back to him. She felt helpless.

"May, look, I love you, and one day, we ain't got to do this no more."

I always listened to May Esther talk as if her own life doesn't exist. She day dreams alot and talks about going places all over the world I hadn't ever heard before. It was like she was in a box with no key.

"Nicky, life is more than this. Ever since I was a little girl, I wanted more…more than what I had."

"May, baby, listen. All that's good, but you're grown now. We got to live the life we have. Deal with the hand that life dealt us."

"Nicky, I don't believe you, and I'm tired," May Esther stood up and got dressed. She stared at herself in the mirror and closed her eyes to keep from crying. May Esther with her tall, lanky body, the shape of a grown woman and her skin the color of milk, had eyes that were blood shot red from cryin' and pleading with Nicky. She pulled her stringy, wet hair back into a long ponytail and wiped her eyes. As she stared into the mirror, she said out loud to herself, "I will one day leave, I love Nicky. I think…well, I did before he turned me into a slave. I pray all the things I want are out there and I'll prove Nicky wrong."

Chapter 4

~

Mama

"Candace! Lord, it's so good to see you and Dre today. It's so hot I didn't think anybody would cross over that road in that sun, but I'm so glad you did. Dre, look at you, Shug, you getting so big. Give mama some sugah," says mama. Then, mama looks at me and whispers, "Can he hear me?"

"Yes mama he just don't say words." I answer her, trying not to sound frustrated, but it's hard to visit mama sometimes." I love her so much, but she looks at Dre like he ain't got good sense. I know she wanted more for me, and I know she loves him. I reckon it's hard for her to understand what's going on with him; the Lord knows I don't. Mama wanted me to be married, but it didn't happen that way. Dre is here, and I will do all I can to make sure he lives a good life. Mama and papa made sure that I had all I needed to get by in life. I guess mama had dreams for me, but I'll never know what they were now that Dre is here. Maybe she feels it's too late.

I had to help mama tend to Ms. Agnes and her husband days when I was young. As soon as I got old enough to learn how to clean, I was brought on. Ms. Agnes would say, "That gal need to be in school." mama would pay her no mind. Mama is strong in her own way, right and proud. Tall and stout and hides it in a flowered housedress every day. She smells like the sweet smell of Jergens lotion when she can buy it, and keeps her hair in an upsweep. She is beautiful.

"Mama, what you been doin'? You feelin' alright?"

"Yeah, Shug, I'm fine, other than these ole knees keep bothering me, but I rub them with that liniment just to ease the ache."

"I smelled it before you got to the door."

We both laughed. I took a deep breath, fixin' to tell mama the news.

"Mr. Harry from the factory let me go, mama."

"What?? That ole dog. He needs anybody he can get to help ship that mess. What you gonna do, Shug? I believe they are looking for folk where Ms. Mamie works at the laundry place up by Camp Lejeune.

"Mama, I'm stuck. I'm only twenty-five with one child who won't talk. My life feels like I'm readin' about it, and not livin' it."

"Candace, look, we didn't have a lot, but me and your Pa did the best we could…you never gone hungry. Ms. Agnes treated us so nice, and I believe she wanted to do right by you. So what we didn't have, she made sure she gave it to us. That woman loved you like you were her own. When you couldn't go to school 'cause you had to help out at her house, she taught you how to read and write. We both prayed the same kinda prayer for you, I'm sure of it. You gonna be all right."

"I'm scared, mama." I started cryin' and realized this is the first time I cried in front of her in a good while. It broke mama's heart to see me cry.

"Oh no, not now. And not in front in that baby. The Good Lord doesn't make mistakes. We all are here for a reason."

"Mama, what if they take Dre away from me?"

Mama lifts her head from cleanin' the stove and looked at me with meanness. "Ain't nobody gonna take Dre away, and don't you ever say that again. Why would they, baby? Stop thinking that way. I know you remember Ms. Agnes walking through the house singin' and prayin' about hope. That's all she had and that's all we have—the same hope…all other ground is sinking sand. And we ain't sinking." mama laughs while she rubs her sore knees, and said, "You know, baby, 'if you got your health, you got everything.' Don't forget that."

Mama makes sense like she always does. I watch Dre turn the pages in the paper at least 100 times in the front room as I lay on the chair. I guess I am so tired from all that's been goin' on. All that thinking I do all day. I hear mama playing with Dre tryin' to get him to say something, but I pretend I am asleep. Before she walked back into the kitchen to finish supper, I felt her hands rub my head a few times. I believe she prayed for me in that moment.

Chapter 5

Ms. Agnes

I couldn't ask mama for one red cent.
I never wanted her to know I couldn't take care of myself. This place ain't bad. Well, I mean, my home ain't bad. It's mine and at least I have a roof over my head. Ms. Agnes left this house for me when she died. She always loved when I came over and took care of her after mama stopped working for her 'cause of her knees. Ms. Agnes would say things like, "What am I gonna do with this big house?"

It was hard for her to come up and down the steps, so after she was bedridden, I would bathe and feed her. I felt sorry for her when she got sick. She was always at Union Stone Baptist singing and helping with Sunday school class. She was a busy woman. Everybody loved her. She treated all the colored people so nice. The young colored boys would tend to her yard and plant flowers for her. She loved sittin' on the big porch rocking back an' forth on her swing reading her Bible. With all the books she had in here, she would read the Bible everyday.

Her husband died a while back, but his heart was not like Ms. Agnes'. She would say, "He is mean as a snake and can't even wipe hisself." He used to beat her, and I never understood why. They had land, this big house, went to church, and had plenty of money. All things that would make you happy, I thought. I got that thinking from mama.

One day I asked mama why he beat on her and she said, "Sometimes, people want more than they have and think you're responsible for them not having it." I guess that's how Nicky feels about May Esther, but he never hit her.

Most colored folks in the south, after the abolition of slavery, wouldn't dare look after White people if they didn't have to. Ms. Agnes was different. I know that she loved me. If she was alive, I believe she could make Dre say words. She talked to me so much. I would listen to her, and I felt I was the smartest girl in the world. She would say, "Never let anybody tell you what you cannot do. After slavery, baby, you colored people can do whatever you want, and be whatever you want to be."

I sometimes found it strange coming from her 'cause she was White. But in my eyes, Ms. Agnes was the truth I needed in my life.

I loved cleaning her bookshelves. They were huge and stretched across the wall. She had thousands of books. It would take me all day. I would take each one and wipe it and put back in its place. They were in order from the smallest to the biggest books. I would come over and read to her some days. In her later years, I would read her Bible, and she would lay there and smile 'till she fell off to sleep. I guess not being able to do the things that made her happy broke her heart; and it gave out on her.

Her spirit and love are in this house. I feel it. Dre grabs a book from the shelves every day and turns the pages, like he is really reading. I hope and pray he will.

Chapter 6

Ms. Pearl

I'clare the days are getting shorter. It's Sunday morning, and Dre won't let the tail of my dress go. Sometimes, I think he wants to say something, but he makes this humming sound all day and night. After church, I usually sit outside, watch people walk, and let Dre kick the dirt up and chase ants. I fret at times that both the White and colored people around here resent me because of this house Ms. Agnes left me. This big white house with the porch wrapped around, which was once owned by White people. She loved me enough to make sure I had a place to call home. I paid them no mind if they were gossiping about me. It's a home for me and my boy. A few colored people live way up the road, but mostly Whites live round here. May Esther is colored but pass for White and Nicky all White, and they are right across the way from me. They don't bother her much about being with a White man because she looks White. She doesn't tell too many people, scared of how she would be treated. I love her and don't care either way what she is or what she can pass for.

"Hey, Ms. Pearl! How you handlin' this heat?" I asked.

Ms. Pearl laughed and says, "Well, you walk fast enough, it can feel like a warm fan. Hey there, Mr. Dre."

Dre looks down at her swollen feet and runs away. I tell him to say hi 'cause she may tell about his silence.

Ms. Pearl is a sweet old White woman who was close friends with Ms. Agnes. I used to tend to her too and still do sometimes. She never had chillun either.

"Candace, what you do all day in this big ole house by yourself? Ain't you lonesome?" She is nosey too.

"No, ma'am. I work most days and Dre be at mama's. No, ma'am, I don't be lonesome."

"Dre ain't in school, Candace?"

"No, Ma'am," I said. "I would wait until next year, being that he is so clingy to me and all."

"Gal, you better let him get used to people. He doesn't know how to talk 'cause you don't talk to him. He needs the company of other chillun' around him."

I almost fell out of my chair when she said that. How did she know and who could have told her? Mama? I try not to act too shocked, but I was. "Well, Ms. Pearl, Dre may have some problems, but he alright, right here with me. He gonna be fine. He still a baby. He will learn it all one day. Ms. Agnes used to tell me: 'Learn all you can from whomever you can learn it from, 'cause nobody owns knowledge.'"

Ms. Pearl chuckled. "Yes, I heard her say that so many times." She made her way up my steps to sit in the rocking chair. Dre was sittin' on the steps with me, eatin' peanut butter crackers. I wish she would leave. I ain't ready for her to tell me how to raise my youngin. "Ooh, the steps make my ankles crack, they so steep, and so many."

Oh no, that means she gonna stay long.

"Candace, you don't know this, but Agnes talked about you all the time. She loved you very much." She finally made it over to that rocking chair. "I never forgot what she told me about you. When you were a little worker with your mama, it hurt her so bad that you couldn't go to school because she thought you were so smart. If you could clean this house and make sure dinner was served at the age of twelve, she knew the potential. Do you know what potential means?"

I liked when Ms. Pearl told how much Ms. Agnes loved me. She swung them short legs, but she was cute as a button. She reminded me of Ms. Agnes, but she was not as kind as Ms. Agnes was. But Ms. Pearl had softened up some. She used to be hateful and snapped words at you that would cut like a knife. I reckoned as she was older now and she ain't got nobody to look after her. I felt sorry for her sometimes.

"I loved Ms. Agnes, sho' 'nuff did…I think about her all the time like she right in the house with me. I wish she could've met Dre. If she held on a little while longer, she would have seen him."

"Now look, I am gonna send someone over here next week so she can meet you and Dre. She is a smart lady and she young. She is about twenty-five years old. People see things in her. God gave her special gifts."

I knew she was going to tell me how to raise my boy. "Ms. Pearl, I know your heart is in the right place, but Dre will be fine.

I just haven't had the time to teach him; that's all. I pray for my baby morning and night. I am always talking to the Lord about my boy and he is going to be okay."

"Alright, Candace, I may be pushing things a bit, but don't you want to hear your baby say 'mama', huh? It will be like music to your ears."

Everything inside of me froze. I wanted to fall to the ground. I felt weak. The thought of Dre saying mama to me almost made me faint.

"Ms. Pearl, that day will come. I don't want nobody trying to say I can't take care of my child. Please, ma'am, just leave that be. We will be fine." I looked at Dre and thought to myself, Oh, how I would love to hear him scream 'mama'!

Chapter 7

"When You Can't Help Yourself"

"Candy!"

"Lord, May, you scared me! What's wrong with you?"

"Look, I need to talk to you."

May Esther looked worn out like she had no energy.

"What happened?" I asked her.

"I can't do it no more, I can't," she said and she was crying so bad, leaning over the porch railing. I ain't never seen May cry. She was always so calm and full of stuff to say. She never told me what goes on at her house, and I ain't never asked.

"Come, Shug, let's go inside. Dre's with mama this morning. It's gonna be okay, May." I was nervous myself. I didn't know what happened, and it was before noon and she was so upset. May sat down and started to wipe her eyes. She stared me in the face and said, "I'm tired. I give myself to men who don't care nothin' for me.

Nicky sits back and let them come at me any kind of way for money. He says I can stop soon, but I can't take it. I got to get away."

I was so confused about May. "Where is Nicky?"

"He ain't home, but I have to leave before he gets back."

"You know this is the first place he will look, May."

May looks at me for answers that I would usually get from her. I feel so bad, 'cause I ain't got nothin' to help. "Candy, my life is hard, but it ain't always been though. I never thought I would give my body to strange men and let 'em treat me like an animal. I take in three or four a day and give Nicky all the money. Every penny. At first, I thought when I started that it would help us live better and get a nice house and a car. And save for me to go to nursing school."

I'd never thought of grown folk wanting to go to school. Ms. Agnes always wanted me to go to school, but I didn't know she meant when I grew up too. I thought May had been to school. I learned from her just sitting on the porch talking.

May stood up and walked to the window peeping out the curtain rubbin' the hair back out of her eyes. I guessed she was looking out for Nicky. "Ain't no more home for me. When my folks told me to leave Nicky alone or get out, I left. Nicky told me the things that every woman wants to hear. He came from a good stock. His daddy a farmer and owned a lot of land. His mama made clothes for the rich White people. He's the only child, and he didn't want to be a farmer like his daddy. He had plans for us to travel. He said 'Let's get rich and travel the world…. He would say 'Let's go to Africa, Egypt, hell, let's go to New York City.'"

May laughed but there wasn't no joy in her eyes.

I couldn't stop looking at her like she was glass. All I could think of was Ms. Agnes saying the same thing to me: "Go out in the world and sightsee life the best you can." Maybe that's what Nicky had in store for May…the best way they could.

I knew the nosey folks around here would soon find out about May if they hadn't already. I was the only one she fools with. I didn't want May to feel worse than what she felt. I never had to give anyone advise on how to live they life. I felt right sorry for her. I wanted her to be well, but I sure didn't want her to leave town. We were close as sisters, but we kept secrets from each other. I didn't tell her about Dre not being able to talk, and she never told me about her secret life with strange men. Mama sometimes asked about May as if she already knew something wasn't quite right with her. I know she has family here in the south. I just prayed that May found what she called peace of mind. We would sit on the porch and stare at the big oak tree in front my house and watch the birds land on the branches. She would say, "I wonder why some birds land on a safe place on a branch and soon after flies away. I wish I was like a bird…to have the wings to fly away even when I am comfortable. I always loved watching birds fly, Candace."

I listened to her as she made sense to herself, but I didn't get it. May looked at me after saying that and smiled. I smiled back, but I don't know what to say. We didn't say anything to each other. In that moment, I knew I was supposed to learn something. I hope one day I will get it. I looked out at the big oak tree and saw the birds come and go. I couldn't never tell if it was the same bird. All from what May Esther said, it sounded like free from worry. That is the peace she wants. Me too.

Chapter 8

A Way Out

Nicky and I never talked. Every time I saw him, he always running, like he's late for something. May loved him, but just didn't like the way they lived.

"May, May!" Nicky shouted. "Where you at?" He ran to the back of their house.

"What, Nicky I'm outside with Candace." May Esther turned to me, wiping her eyes. "Candy, I gotta go, but I will be back. I need your help...."

May walked in the house. Nicky was sitting on the floor sweating like a pig. His face was red and his black, curly hair was wet like after a fresh rain. May sat beside him and rubbed his back, waiting for him to tell her what's wrong.

"Honey, we got to leave here. I got myself into something I can't get out of...betting on the chicken fights."

"What happened, Nicky? I don't want to run and hide no more. I can't even walk outside from shame. If we gonna leave, I want to leave for a better life. Not leave and live the same way."

"A better life?" Nicky stood in a rage and says, "What kind of better life? You living here, eat well, and I buy you anything you want."

"You buy it with my money, Nicky. I can't even go to the store for a nab and coke unless I ask you for money." It seemed like May finally had enough. "I want to stop this, Nicky. I am hurting on the inside. I can't feel no more."

Nicky looked at her with pity. He got a soft spot for May. I think he loved her, but things just wasn't the way he expected. "May, I owe some money out and I can't pay it all back. These guys are rough city boys from Chicago. They may try to kill me."

May jumped up, looking scared. She hesitated to ask a question because she was scared what the answer was gonna be. "We ain't got no money? *No* money? The way I sold my body to those dirty bastards to do better…it's gone, ain't it, Nicky?" May charged after him, screaming and crying, hitting him in the back. All Nicky could do is block her hits and look away.

"It happened so fast, May. I wanted to tell you, I 'clare I did but I got in too deep. I lost it before I realized it was gone."

May grabbed her purse and sweater and started toward the door. Nicky grabbed her arm. May didn't put up a fight.

Her dreams of going to nursing school, getting married, raising kids, and traveling the world… were all lies. Lies Nicky fed May to keep her satisfied. I guess after that, May was downright disappointed. She ain't stay around Nicky too much after that.

"I'm leaving. I'll be back. I just…can't feel anything right now…not even anger."

He let go of her arm, stepped back, and says, "I got dreams too. I got a plan for us. You'll see."

"No, I won't Nicky we are slowly sinking, sinking. I've been used, beat, and lied to most of my life. You were the only one I had left. I thought all those nights we dreamt together, the money I put in your hands…blood money, *blood money!*" May started screaming at the top of her lungs and crying. "I'll back be, Nicky. I need to think alone and see if the Lord will hear my prayer."

Nicky turned around and walks toward the front door. He screamed, "May, I got a plan, May!"

When May didn't make him no answer, he knew he'd messed up. He lied down on the floor mumblin' to himself, "I'm so sorry."

Nicky never knew what was hurting May Esther all those years. She didn't know what to do or, many times, what to say. She never told him what she felt. He laid there for hours hoping May would come back so he could try to make things right.

Chapter 9

Minding My Business

Mama didn't live that far from me but far enough. Every time I walked fast, it felt like a bone was trying to break through my back. Ms. Agnes would get on me about having aches and pains. She'd say, "Baby, you are too young to have body aches." I guess she never thought I could ache after lifting her up and down off that sick bed, weighing almost much as a horse.

I wondered what mama cooked. Since I was not working, I tried to hold on to whatever meat and beans I had until I found work again. I got close to the house and saw mama and Dre outside, talking to a strange White woman on her porch. Dre sitting still, and I couldn't believe my eyes. Mama could get any child to sit still, even mine.

"Hey, Shug," mama yells down the road, waving. I couldn't wait to see what this White woman was talkin' about. Maybe she's trying to get mama to change her religion like they did with Grandma, mama's mother. I feel sorry for her if she was trying to change her mind because mama will sho tell her, "There is one God and you can't change that, no matter what you'll put together."

Dre looked up and ran straight to me.

"Hey, bumble bee, been a good boy?"

Dre always rubbed my back or punched it. That was his way of speaking to me or trying to get me to give him something he wants.

"Hey, mama," I said and looked at the White woman; she was blind. I felt a little funny because I'd never met a blind person before. I couldn't even imagine what mama was doin' talking to her. I bent over to kiss mama while Dre was holdin' on to my dress. "Candace, this here is Ms. Ferby," mama says.

Ms. Ferby looked toward me and reached out her hand. "Howdy, Ms. Candace? I've heard so much about you. I feel like I know you already. Your boy here is filled with energy and is very charismatic."

I listened to her in shock. I had never heard that word before either. I smiled even though she can't see me. "Thank you, ma'am." I looked over at mama and she was lookin' at me like she did something wrong.

"Baby, Ms. Ferby is a teacher down at Edney Chapel schoolhouse. Ms. Pearl told her about Dre not speaking and all."

I didn't know whether to march to Ms. Pearl's porch and tip over that rocking chair she always in or just scream. My heart was racing so fast, I didn't know what to say. I looked at mama and made a face. She looked back at me and shrugged her shoulders. I grabbed my bag of food and grabbed Dre by the hand so we could get out of there. "It's nice to have met you, ma'am, but we got to get back down the road before dark."

"I know you thinkin' all kinds of things right now, Candace, but I believe in the power of God, and I know He's blessed me with gifts to help children."

I looked at Ms. Ferby from her head to her toes as she couldn't see me. She was a tall, thin lady with stringy blonde hair. The heat didn't help none either. She holdin' that seeing stick like we depend on our eyes. Seemed young to be a teacher, must've been smart. Ms. Agnes would've wanted me to talk to her. I reckoned she would. Mama was sippin' on iced tea as the ice melts, lookin' at me and making hand signals to me. She expected me to say something else to Ms. Ferby but I ain't sure what else to say.

"Candy, baby, she said Dre can learn and may be able to even talk one day," mama said as if she knew for sure. "You know, Sis. Erma from the church always believed her daughter would come home from that hospital. Cause you know she couldn't see or talk. But God made a way. Now she helps make quilts with yarn and a needle. She sews just as good as we ole ladies do on Sunday afternoons."

I didn't know why mama was telling me all this. I was still saying no. "Ms. Ferby, I must be going, but thank you for being interested in my boy. I will have more time to teach Dre since I don't work anymore. Thank you for caring. I know Ms. Pearl meant well, but we will be just fine." I looked around for Dre, and he was sittin' in the dirt hummin' to himself and kicking the dirt away.

"I understand, Ms. Candace. I want to tell you one thing if you don't mind. The hummin' sound Dre makes soothes him and it's natural in children who can't speak. I'm sure he does it often, and if so, it's okay. Well, let me get on my way too. Good day, ladies."

I felt so sad that I couldn't pull a word out of him. It felt right when she talked to me though, 'cause I didn't know what that hummin' meant. "Dre, come on, bumble bee." He jumped up and I looked to the sky. Thank God that he can at least hear me.

"Mama, I'm gonna drop Dre off early in the morning to see if I can get work at the warehouse in town."

Ms. Ferby stepped down and grabbed her school bag. She started off a little, then turned around, and said, "Ms. Candace I know you sayin' how am I going to help if I'm blind. But God gave me sumthin' only He can give, and that is a desire and wisdom to teach children. All types of children. Even blind children like me. Ms. Agnes used to tell me that same thing."

I stopped Ms. Ferby and said, "You knew Ms. Agnes?"

"Yes, I did, very well. She used to be my Sunday school teacher when I was young. Ms. Agnes was a beautiful human being. She wasn't like most people. She taught me when they told my mama I couldn't be taught."

Ms. Ferby was standing there with the biggest smile on her face. I started thinking about all the talks me and Ms. Agnes used to have. I never thought I was smarter than she said I was. That's why Ms. Agnes was so smart; she even taught the blind to see with their mind and heart.

"I was young and I didn't know Ms. Agnes was a teacher like that. I used to wonder why she had so many books all over the house, but to teach a—"

Ms. Ferby interrupts me with, "—teach a blind person?"

"I reckon," I say.

Mama went into the house to get papa's supper together, and came back to the door and asked if I want to stay for supper so I won't have to cook nothin' up.

"No, ma'am, I'm going to go now." I reached to shake Ms. Ferby's hand and grabbed it gently. "Good evening, ma'am, and thank you for giving me such good memories of Ms. Agnes. I feel her spirit every day in that big house." I avoid talking about Dre.

Ms. Ferby called out to Dre, and to my surprise, he went right over to her. Dre pushed her leg and ran back to grab my hand. "He doesn't hug nobody, so that was his way of saying bye."

We both laughed. This has been so much to take in. On my walk home, I wondered how Ms. Agnes taught a blind person. She was the smartest person in the world.

Chapter 10

~

May Esther: No Looking Back

I hate when it rains. The roof is so old that it doesn't take much for the water to come through. Then the water drips all night, until it stops. The wooden bucket catching the water done filled up. I reckon some of the White people walk by and wonder why Ms. Agnes gave me this house, and think I'm not going to keep it pretty. She felt love for me, as if I was her own. Mama would sometimes get upset 'cause she paid me so much mind.

    I needed to try to empty out that bucket of water while I can carry it. This house was so quiet sometimes, almost spooky. I needed to get more firewood from papa. That lamp was burning so hot, and I was trying not to drop it walking up those steps. It was a good day to clean out all that stuff in that attic. Ms. Agnes never cleaned up here, and neither did I. So many boxes filled with books and old clothes. They lived here so long; they couldn't help but save stuff....

    What in the world was that noise? I thought suddenly. It sounded like a mouse back there. I hope not. I couldn't take those things. If Dre found it, he'd wanna try to play with it. *Let me just pull a few boxes out and see what's goin' on*, I thought.

"Ahhh!" I screamed and jumped back.

"It's me, Candace! I didn't mean to scare you." It was May Esther whisperin' like she was hidin' from somebody.

She scared me half to death. "May Esther, what in heaven's name are you doing up here? Gal, you scared me crazy. What's wrong, May?"

"Candace, I'm hiding from Nicky."

"What has he done to you?"

May looked really pale. Like she hadn't eaten or slept for days.

"Come on downstairs. We gonna get you cleaned up and make you supper. But first, help me dump out this bucket out the window." I started reachin' for the bucket, but May wasn't moving toward it.

"I can't let Nicky see me, Candace."

I didn't know what's going on, but I was scared for May. She never seemed scared about anything. What could Nicky have done to her for her to run off and make her leave her own home? I pushed the bucket of water to the window, and sure 'nuff there was Nicky, walking down the street and smokin' a cigarette.

"May, Nicky just left the house. He is walking down the street, heading for Mr. Gus' store," I reported to May.

"He's coming back, Candace; he is looking for me."

She started crying and unable to control it. I pushed the boxes out the way and put a blanket around her. She was so pitiful, I'd never seen her like this before. She pulled me down to the floor next to her and said, "Nicky gets all the money from me, and done gambled it away betting on chicken fights. It was my dream money that I thought was put away for us.... Now it's all gone, Candace, and they looking to hurt him or kill him I suppose. He came home yesterday scared to death, crying and begging me to leave town with him. He is running from the killers."

I sat there in shock, my mind all over the place. "I will fix you something to eat and get you cleaned up. I know you been cold up here with the rain and all." I helped her up and went downstairs. She was silently crying and moaning. *I'll come back up and empty that darn bucket,* I thought. *Maybe I can get papa to come or Uncle Doug to do it.*

Chapter 11

Lost Nicky

"Dammit, May! Come back please. Where you at, May? I's so sorry."

Nicky was walking up and down the road, screaming out for May. I was watching him and listening from the upstairs window, peeking out the curtain. He started to walk to my house and stops suddenly. A car stopped next to him, and I can hear Nicky say as I listened out of my side window. "Hey man, whats going on?

"Nicky you look bad man, like you got hit by a truck," the person in the car said.

"Dan, I messed up. I owe them punks some money, and now I have to run off before they kill me."

"I told you so many times them White boys don't mess around Nick. Even if you White, they will still kill you." Dan was one of the hustlers makin' that homemade liquor. They sat out there under that tree on the other road drinking all day and night. "Nicky, you got to work something out with them." Get May to work all night some days.

Nicky looked towards his house, and Dan parked the car and got out to smoke a cigarette. "She left me…I can't find her. I told her what happened, and she slipped out on me. I came home and all her things were gone." Nicky looked downright bad. I almost felt sorry for him. Seemed like he really missed May.

"May Esther was the best thing that happened to me. She was my rock, and I used her like a ragdoll. She wasn't no normal woman. She had dreams and I killed each one," Nicky went on.

Dan put out his cigarette and says, "Man, you got to let her go and find you another one."

He just sat there daydreaming, thinking of a way to get out of this mess. "Hey, Dan," he then said, "can you carry me uptown? I might see her."

Chapter 12

May Esther's Way Out

May Esther had been at my house for a week now. It felt nice having company, even though we couldn't sit on the porch and talk. She was so scared Nicky would see her. He came by here twice in the middle of the week. Of course, I didn't answer the door. I wasn't scared of him, but I was scared for May Esther. May didn't want anyone to know she was here. Not even mama.

She asked me to call her sister from my mama house. She lived in Georgia. She told me to ask her sister to send for her. I left the house and prayed that I wouldn't run into Nicky on the way to mama's. I was glad mama was gone when I got there, so she wouldn't ask so many questions. I was so nervous to call May's sister but I had to call.

"Hi, ma'am. My name is Candace, I am a friend of your sister May Esther," I told over the phone.

She got quiet and said, "Lord, is May alright?" She sounds proper to live in the country. I almost couldn't understand her.

"Yes, ma'am, she wants you to send for her."

She interrupted me with, "What's wrong with her? Is Nicky with her? Why hasn't she called me? I haven't heard from her in months. I been worried sick about her."

I couldn't get a word in from her asking one question after another."

"Well, ma'am, May needs to get away and wanted you to send for her. She needs to leave Nicky, and you her only chance, ma'am."

She was quiet and seemed confused about what I was saying to her. May had told her family she was here going to school and that Nicky been working on a farm, tendin' to horses. She wanted them to think they were living good and had money saved up. I wasn't tellin' her no different either. I gave her mama's address and asked her to send a letter right away or send a wire.

"Honey I didn't get your name. Honey, what is your name? I'm sorry if you already told me. Can you tell me again?"

"My name is Candace."

"How do you know my sister, honey? Did you go to school with her?"

That felt good hearing her ask if I went to school with May. I cleared my throat and stopped daydreamin' long enough to answer her. "No, ma'am; we live on the same road."

"Well, I want to speak to May. I trust what you're saying is the truth, honey, but I would feel better if I heard it from May Esther."

I didn't know what to say then. "Yes, ma'am, I know you do, but May is a bit scared to be seen by Nicky. They fallin' apart and May needs to leave town. I would let you talk to my mama if you don't believe me, ma'am, but she ain't home just yet." I sho' didn't want mama to know any of this.

She stopped talkin' I thought she passed out.

"Ma'am are you there? Can you hear me?" I asked.

"Yes, honey, I'm here. I just don't understand, and I am a little afraid."

"Maybe I can sneak May Esther over here one evening when no one will notice, so you can talk to her."

She was relieved when I told her that. "That would be a blessing if you could. I just don't want to be fooled by sending money to a stranger."

"Yes, ma'am, I am going back and tell her how you feel."

"Please tell May Esther I'm praying for her, and I love her."

"Yes, ma'am, I will." I didn't know how this was going to happen.

I needed to pray right now that The Lord will answer May Esther's prayers.

CHAPTER 13

Ms. Ferby and Ms. Pearl

On the way back to my house, I was so nervous though I didn't know why. I reckoned it's 'cause I hadn't ever had this much business going on. I didn't know how to get May to mama's without Nicky seeing her. Mama walked in and heard me talking to May's sister. The first thing mama yelled out after I hung up: "I don't want no mess, Candace! Helping might only hurt." I couldn't believe that it would hurt.

Oh no. Just then, I see Ms. Ferby and Ms. Pearl sitting on Ms. Pearl's porch. I heard Ms. Pearl yelling for me like a wild woman. I wished someone would chase me so I can run right past her house. "Hey, ma'am! Hey, Ms. Ferby. I'm rushing off to get to Dre. Can't really talk now."

But Ms. Pearl made three attempts to get up from the one-sided rocking chair before she said, "Candace, come here, honey, just for a spell. I want to check with you about something."

Goodness, they'd been talking about Dre again, I thought. I wasn't gonna do it. I was okay with Dre for now. She could say all she wants. I got close to the steps but didn't sit down like she asked me to. "Hey, Ms. Ferby; it sure is a hot day today. I reckon it may rain."

Ms. Ferby was sittin', movin' her head from side to side. She looked pretty today, her skin, so clear and milky. I'd never seen her eyes before 'cause of the dark glasses she wore. "Hi, Ms. Candace! How are you today? You sound as if something took your breath. Where is that handsome boy of yours?"

How does she know he's handsome? There were so many questions I wanted to ask, but I was scared. I was sure she already sensed I didn't know too many things.

"He just fine, jumpy as a rabbit and getting fat as a tick," I replied.

We all laugh together.

Ms. Pearl couldn't seem to wait to say something. She was sittin' an' dippin' snuff. "Candy, Ms. Ferby here means well, and you know I care what happens to you and your youngin. I feel I gotta help because of how Ms. Agnes loved you so. You took care of her when no one would. Not even your mama."

She always had to remind me of that as if I didn't know. I would do anything for Ms. Agnes. Ms. Ferby interrupted me next. I guess she could feel I was about to walk away. "Ms. Candace, do you mind if I stop by and talk to you for a moment? Or you and Dre can stop by the schoolhouse to introduce him to the other children."

That had me stuck. I couldn't open my mouth, and then I hurried and said, "Yes, ma'am, we will show up at the schoolhouse."

I couldn't believe I'd said yes. What was wrong with me? Well, I couldn't take it back. Maybe that was the part of me that was filled with hope. I didn't know it was there, but it made me change my mind. The part of me that was afraid…God was taking it away. I prayed He was.

Ms. Ferby started clapping her hands together with a big smile. "Oh, Ms. Candace; my heart is filled with happiness right now. I thank you so much."

I couldn't say anything back to her. I just walked away feeling confused. Ms. Pearl acted like somebody gave her some food; she was so happy too. My heart felt lighter. I knew takin' Dre to school was the right thing to do, but I was frightened by what it can make him do. How will he act? Will the chillun be scared of him? Will he have one of them fits and they take him to the hospital? I couldn't let them thoughts come on me about the hospital. I didn't believe in my heart God will let them do it, like mama said.

I was praying and walking as fast as I can back to the house. "Lord Jesus, help me with Dre. I know You know it all, but please don't let them take Dre from me, in Jesus' name I pray."

I started to run a little before I realized I didn't say goodbye. *Oh, well, now back to May Esther.* I know Dre got her chasing him all over the house. Lord, help me with May too.

"May Esther, you upstairs?" I walked through the hallway, callin' out to her, "I know Dre wore you out."

Now where in the world are they? I thought. I knew she wouldn't take Dre out the house. The house was clean—no toys on the steps. I was getting a little nervous. *Let me check upstairs* I thought. I was yelling louder now. "Dre, May Esther!" My heart was about to stop. What if Nicky had been here and took them? I was screaming as loud as I could, until I realized I didn't want to say May's name so Nicky can hear me in the back of the house. I ran back in the house, rushed up in the stairs, and started toward the attic.

I heard a faint noise, and listened for a minute, and then screamed "May" as loud as I can. This house is so big it felt like a puzzle. May Esther came to the top of the attic steps and told me to shush. "Dre is sleep."

"May! You scared the craziness out of me. Why did you bring him up here? It's so dark and dreary!" I got up to the attic and looked around, and it was spotless up there. Just dust and old smells from the water leaking through the roof. May Esther had pushed all of Ms. Agnes' boxes to the side and made a bed out of the old quilts Ms. Virginia, Ms. Bersie, and Ms. Agnes made.

I look to the side by the wall; Dre was sound asleep. I couldn't believe my eyes. He got clean pajamas on and was smellin' so good, with Wildroot in his hair. "Candace, I couldn't keep still. You know I've been a nervous wreck since you left to call my sister. I made Dre a bath in the bucket out back and brought him up here to read one of the books to him."

I was in amazement that she read to him. I didn't know if I should be mad or happy.

"I can't believe it, May! What did he do when you read to him?"

"I declare, Candace, he sat there and listened like I was feeding him jelly cakes. Every time I stopped reading, he would hit my hand or touch my mouth to keep going. He loved the books,

Candace. If he can sit and listen like he did tonight, he smart, Candace. Smarter than you think. He just need a little help with sittin' still," May Esther said and laughed.

I sat on the floor with tears in my eyes and started rubbing his head.

"I'm sorry, Candace. Please don't cry. This is God's way of showing you he's gonna be okay. I know you worried, but he was happy. He kept running over to the boxes and pullin' all the books."

I smiled and wondered what it all meant. Maybe that blind lady Ms. Ferby was right. Maybe he can learn. I never once thought to pull out any books for Dre to read to him, and there are so many on the book shelves downstairs. What did it all mean?

Chapter 14

Desperation

After dealing with Dre, I put him in the bed after a night of reading. It feels so good to even say that. May sitting in my room, waitin' for me to come tell her about what happened with the call to her sister.

"What my sister say? Is she gonna send the money? I know she had so many questions. What did you tell her?" May was talking so fast I couldn't get nothin' out. I couldn't answer one question before she asked another one.

"She was a little shocked that I called, but she wants to talk you for herself, May."

"Candace, I can't leave. I *cannot* leave this house. Nicky will find me," May said and stood up, and then fell to her knees, crying and shaking. I rubbed her hair and tried to calm her before she wakes Dre.

"May, your sister doesn't know me. She won't send the money to a stranger. She real nice about it, but she wants to hear your voice."

May didn't know what to do now. She wiped her eyes and got up from the floor. There were days when she was feelin' comfortable hiding from Nicky, but now she felt fear and like she was trapped.

We both were not sure what to do, so I told May to put firewood in the stove, to warm up the house a bit. May cut me off as I walked by her and said, "Candace, you may not like what I'm going to say, but it's my only chance. I can't leave this house to call my sister, and I ain't got no money. And you don't either. Look, I must entertain a man. One last time."

I never thought she would say that, never. I looked at her as if she lost her mind. I didn't even know exactly what to say. "May, you said you hated that life. Please don't. Maybe my mama can help a little or papa.

May screamed, "No! Please, Candace! I need you to do this. Can he please come here for a few hours? He an old bastard. It won't take long. Then I will have the money to leave here and start a new life. It's my only hope."

She sounded desperate. I know she was not thinking straight. She was just begging and grabbing my arms with force. My mind was everywhere, but I couldn't let her do that here. I was sure the nosey people around here knew what Nicky and May had been doing. *Lord Jesus, help me! I cannot let this go on in Ms. Agnes house. Even though it's my house now, her spirit ain't never left* I thought. Ms. Agnes hated when her husband drank that corn liquor in the house. She would say, "I pray and worship in this house, and you won't turn it into a whiskey barn." I can only imagine what she would say if I let May do this.

Or mama, if she found out. "Candace, you ain't working, and you could use the money to buy clothes for Dre and food."

"I 'clare, May, I'm gonna have to pray about it. I want you to get away too, but my baby is here in this house. And mama would kill me if she even thought that company was for me."

"You are right, Candace." She kept walking up the stairs and then said, "Goodnight, see you in the morning."

Chapter 15

A New Day

"Dre, baby, wake up. It's time to go see mama." From the minute he opens his eyes, he got so much energy. I needed to see about a job that morning. I hated to think I had to clean up after someone again. I just ain't gonna do it.

Oh shoot, I should have said my prayers before I woke him up, I thought and wondered if God heard my prayers if I was not on my knees. I know it's a sign of respect when you are on your knees while praying.

"Lord Jesus, thank you for waking me and Dre up this mornin'. Thank you for the light that shines on our face. Can You please show me what to do about Dre? There is something special about him. Please bless mama and papa and take away the pain that May Esther is feelin'. Free her from Nicky. In Jesus' name I pray. Amen."

So much going on in my life, I believe He will hear me and answer my prayers. Hope is all I'm standing on.

I walked out on the porch after I gave Dre his grits. It was a nice day. *Maybe I will go to the factory and see if they are hiring,* I thought. *Oh, let me check on May.*

I walked through the kitchen, lookin' for Dre. He must've run to the attic after those books. If May Esther was asleep, he'd wake her up by runnin' up the stairs. When I found Dre, he was just turning the pages in the book. May was gone. All her bags gone and she'd put up the quilts where she'd made a bed. I must have pushed her away. I felt awful. I saw that Dre was playing with a piece of paper and walked over to see what it was; it was from May.

"Candace, I will be back real soon. Thank you for being my friend. I hope to be like you one day. I'm gonna be fine. God is with me, and I have hope. Love you and Mighty Dre. I left the book out for Dre. Please read to him every day. Go see the blind teacher too. Dre needs to learn so much more." —May Esther

It was hard to imagine that I may never see May Esther again. I was shocked and scared for May. Anything could happen while she was trying to be free from Nicky. I believed May was a lot stronger than I thought she was. Many days we'd sit on the porch, and she would stare into the sky, and tell me, "Candace, I love daydreaming; it makes me imagine my life like I want it to be."

I thought of all the advice I'd been giving about Dre; I'd never thought to think of what I want life to look like for me.

Chapter 16

Surrender

It has been a week since May left, and I hadn't heard a peep from her. I walked to Cagey's store and saw Uncle Jack's drinking buddies sitting in front of the store with their own chair. "Hey there, little lady." His face was red as a beet out there, drinking in this hot weather.

"Hey! Hot day, ain't it?"

"Yeah, it is. Hope the storm come'; will cool it down."

Old folk sho' can tell when a storm is comin'.

I grabbed a couple things for mama and me for the week. I guessed I could cook a little for us instead of always eatin' supper at mama's. I was in line waiting to pay, when I heard the store owner talking about a man got shot on the other road leading into Richlands. I asked the clerk, Ms. Jane, who were they talking about. She was the gossip tree around here.

"They say Nicky got shot. You know, the White boy that had the house not too far from yours."

My heart almost stopped. I instantly thought about May. What if they got her too? I grabbed the bags and said, "Oh my, that's too bad."

I was scared to ask if he was dead, but before I could ask, she yelled out, "He ain't dead, but they chopped one of his hands off. You know they say he owed money for bettin' on those chicken fights. I heard for years that when you owe them people money and don't pay back, they cut your hand off."

I was almost not breathing as I listened. "Okay, I gotta get to mama's for supper."

She had one more thing to say as usual. "Hey have you seen that White-looking gal who was with him?"

"No, ma'am," I ran out the store.

I heard her yell, "Tell your folks I said 'hey.'"

They wanted him dead and he knew it. I was so worried about May. What if she decided to go back to him and they found her too? I couldn't think like that. I wouldn't think like that. I needed to hurry to mama's; I heard the thunder up yonder.

It took a lot of convincing and praying about school for Dre. I felt a little better about it as I couldn't seem to stop him from running in the attic and looking in those books every day. Some of the books had pictures and some didn't. I thought he liked looking at the pictures, but he looked at the books with words the most. I told mama about Dre and the books, and she told me to take him to see the midwife in Jacksonville and see if she could help.

Mama thought Dre was sick or slow. She loved him but she didn't understand his problem.

There was something strange about it all. I read to him every day like May said to do. He listened so good and looked up to the ceiling while I read. He never looked me in the face. He usually looked around like he was thinking about something. I noticed it when he was a baby. Now I notice a whole lot. I wanted to be able to save Dre from life. I wanted no harm to come him because he couldn't talk and acted peculiar.

Chapter 17

Trust

I was about to have a breakdown. I never thought this day would come. I saw Ms. Ferby yesterday on Ms. Pearl's porch, and she told me that the school opened at seven. She told me I could bring Dre as early as I wanted to. I told her I thought I'd stay with him the whole time.

I believed Dre is gonna be scared as a wet cat when he walks in there. I really didn't know how to feel. I prayed before the sun came up that the Good Lord will give me a sign. I heard mama say so many times to sit back and watch the hand of God in your life. I reckoned this was one of those times. I was standing at Dre's bedroom door. My sweet baby was sleeping so peacefully. Neither of us knew what this day would bring.

The minute he opened his eyes, I had to be ready to run and move just as fast as he does. "Dre, Dre, wake up, Shug."

All his toys and strings he plays with were all lined up against the wall. He did it every night before bed. Sometimes it took him half the night. It was a funny thing but he did it the exact same.

"Dre," I said as I move a closer to the bed and rub his hair. Just then, I felt something hard against my foot under the bed. I pull back the quilt to look under the bed, and there were so many books under there. I got on my knees in amazement. They were stacked up one by one from the floor to the tip of the bed. I pulled one of the books out and Dre jumped out the bed, making mumble sounds like he havin' one of those fits. He began to hit his head with his fist. He snatched the book from me before I could get off my knees. I backed up and watched him fix the books, making sure they were straight. He walked around the bed and touched each book, as if he was counting them. They were perfect after he finished.

I noticed all the books started with the same letter in each row. All the b's, t's, and s's. I don't know… it must have been May Esther who set it up like this for him before she left. I didn't know what to think. What if Dre did it?

"That's so nice, Shug…look what you did," I said as I stood. And he ran to me, pushin' his little head into my leg like he always does and left the room. The only way I could hold on to him long enough for a hug was when I play with him for a minute. He'd never been an affectionate child.

Now that I thought about it, Dre must have put those books under the bed. I'd just washed the bed linen the other night when he peed in the bed. I'm sure I would have felt those books then. I decided not to tell mama though. Maybe he saw the books as toys and just wanted to play with them. Some kids have wild imaginations and play with just about anything. They ain't got nothing else to do. That don't mean they crazy.

I played with wooden spoons and acted like they were my baby dolls. Oh, well. Maybe I will tell Ms. Ferby or maybe not. "Dre, come on, Shug. It's time to go to school." I'd never thought I would say.

I was running around like my head cut off making sure Drew was fit for school. He needed a haircut, but I put the Wild Root lotion on it in the meantime. It will make it soft and smell good. I'd have papa cut it after school. I put on his white church shirt and dungaree shorts. He didn't know where he was going, and I was so scared that his happy little life here with me will change for better or make it worse.

I walked into the family room and there he was, sitting in front of the bookcases, taking them out one by one and putting them back. I never noticed he liked the books so much. They were like his new toys. If Ms. Agnes could see Dre touching those books, she would have a natural born fit. She took pride in them books and made sure they were wiped clean every week. One of the chores I hated the most as her maid.

She made sure I would read a book a week as well. She claimed it would help me speak pretty. After she passed, I tried to stick with it, but my mind wouldn't keep focused. As I stood at the screen door looking at Dre, he was just rocking back and forth, looking at the pages. I wanted to see what he would do if I took away from him.

"Dre, time to go up the road to school. Give me the book, Shug." I reached down and tried to take the book slowly.

Dre jumped up, made a loud noise, and ran out the screen door with the book. He ran clear up the road!

I ran fast as I could after him screaming his name. "Dre!" I never lost sight of him. As I get close, a man came around the corner and stopped Dre from crossing the road.

"Dre! Dre!" I began to cry and grabbed Dre from the man. "Thank you, Mister, thank you." I never looked up at the man. I was trying to calm Dre down, while he kicked and pulled away from me. After all this, Dre still wouldn't let go of the book. I couldn't seem to calm him down. I rubbed his head and held him so tightly. He usually calmed down after I hold him tight. He hadn't had a fit like this in a long time.

He hit my hand then tried to bite it. The man stood there looking the whole time. Dre finally got tired of fighting me, and I put him down. I squeezed his hand so tight. The man looked at me with a serious face and said, "You know May Esther?"

I looked up and it was Nicky. But he only had one hand. It was wrapped with white tape from the wrist up. I couldn't speak at first, so I turned around and started back. Then I said, "Thank you for your help, Sir."

He walked behind me and said with a soft voice, "I remember you. You May's friend. Candace. Where is May? Please tell me?"

"I'm sorry, sir, but I don't know."

Nicky looked so bad, beaten up by life. "It's almost a year and I haven't seen or heard from her. I need her so badly, Candace."

I keep walking, almost dragging Dre down the road. I was afraid he would follow me home. He slowed up when he saw a group of children walking to the schoolhouse. They began to run away from Nicky screaming, "That's the man with one hand!"

Nicky yelled down the road at me, "Tell May I love her!"

I didn't know why that morning turned out as it did. *Maybe Dre ain't meant to go to school. Why did I see Nicky and his one hand?* I know Ms. Ferby is going to come to my house tonight worrying me about why I didn't bring Dre to school.

I was too tired to even go upstairs. I reckon I sit here in the family room and watch Dre play with his strings and them books. I kept thinking about Nicky and all that just happened. I couldn't tell mama though. She would want me to come live with her. Papa might tell my Uncle Dan and Uncle Jack, and no tellin' what they would do to him. The only thing that satisfies my heart about today is that May is not with Nicky. It's just what I hoped for. Thank you God!

Chapter 18

Keep Pushing

I didn't know how I'd feel about working now. Dre was older, but with his peculiar ways, people wouldn't understand. He was getting harder to deal with. He hardly listened to me. Last week, he was so upset, 'cause I wouldn't let him go to the attic and pull out them books. He tore the house up, hit himself so hard, and bit his hand. At times I couldn't handle him. I made sure he didn't hurt himself by talkin' calm to him and prayin'. Mama knew he was getting worse, and she wanted to say something, but I reckoned she was scared to. I 'clare I need to work to keep this house up. I didn't really care about school for him right now. Well I just don't know.

Who in the world was at that door? *Oh no!* I thought; it was Ms. Pearl. *Now how did she wobble down so early in the day? The sun ain't even shown its color yet?* "Hey, Ms. Pearl! You beat the sun this morning."

She was breathing so hard liked she'd been chased. She never liked to come in. I guess one more step past the porch chairs were too much. "Whew Lawd, Candace! It is a clear morning, but a walk down that road is too much for an old woman like me. You need to a get that telephone working. Your mama got one." She's started complaining already. After she leaves, I was gonna hide those porch chairs so she won't have to stop in.

"How you feel', Ms. Pearl?" I asked her.

Her feet were so swollen in her white nursing shoes, they looked like they were gonna burst.

"Ms. Ferby told me you didn't show up at the schoolhouse with Dre yesterday. If anybody can help, it is her. I know you thinking how this blind woman could help your son."

"Ms. Pearl, Dre was sick."

"Where is he now? I'm surprised he ain't run out here yet."

"He's asleep now, and I need to get ready to go to work. I don't mean to rush you, but I still need to get breakfast for him."

Just as Ms. Pearl was about to get up and leave, Dre came running out on the porch with two books.

"Hey there, Mr. Dre! Hey, Shug. What you got there?"

Dre took the books over to her and laid them on her lap. He was just turning pages as if he was reading. Ms. Pearl took the book (Dre never took his hand off of it) and said, "Shug, this is a good book."

Dre slapped her hand and pointed to the open page, like he wanted her to start reading. He touched the page so hard, and Ms. Pearl start reading. I could tell she was amazed at how he was listening. Dre began to rock back and forth and stare up to the sky while she read page after page. I needed to stop her so we could get ready. He put his hand on Ms. Pearl's leg while reading. She stopped and looked at me, and I hurried and turned my head.

I ignored her. I didn't want her to know I knew he acted this way about books. But in my heart, I was scared of his ways.

"Well, we done held you long enough. I know you got things you need to do this morning, Ms. Pearl. I have to get ready to start this long day." I didn't want her to know I was taking Dre to school today.

"Candace, you feel okay?"

"Yes. I'm starting a new job today and I need to get there."

"How is your mama? I see your papa every now and then. I reckon he is working on the farm these hot days."

"They fine," I answered as grab Dre's hand and he pulls away. I didn't want to force it, 'cause I didn't want her to see him act out "Ms. Pearl, good to see you. You take care now. I guess I see you as I pass your house on the way church Sunday. I promised mama I would go Sunday."

"Good, Candace, 'cause you know we got to make time for the Lord."

"Yes, ma'am. Mama says it all the time when I don't go."

Finally, she moved, taking a small step at a time, and she was almost gone. She pulled out her hand to shake Dre's hand and tried to give him a hug. Instead, he took the books back in the house. "Candace, you take care of him. You got one special yungin' there." She makes it to the last step, turns around, and says, "God has plans for him; I know it. That's why he's here. All you must do is have hope and faith. God will one day show you all the answers to your questions." And she walked off.

Chapter 19

~

The Test

My hands were so sweaty. I know it looks like I'd been working in the sun. The closer I got to the schoolhouse the more I wanted to drop to the ground. It felt like Dre was walking me to the school; he was holding my hand so tightly. Often times, I wondered what he thought of me if he could talk.

We were almost there because I could see the big white school sign in the yard: "Edney Chapel." I was humming as I walked with him and slowed down a bit to calm him before he saw the children playin' in the sandbox.

He looked up at me and I started singing, "Great is thy faithfulness, great is thy faithfulness. Morning by morning our mercies are new. All that I needed God have provided."

Dre pulled away from me and ran toward the school yard. "Dre!" I screamed, "Come back! Wait!"

He jumped right into the sandbox and sat with two boys about his age. "Dre!" One of the little boys jumped out and ran into the school. A teacher, I supposed, walked out of the school onto the porch and looked at me trying to pull Dre out of the sandbox. Then she said in a soft kind voice, "He's okay; he can stay."

I looked at her and looked down. I wasn't expecting anybody else except Ms. Ferby. I reckoned she needed help with the children. "Can I help you, ma'am?" she asked. I wiped my face off with the handkerchief from my pocket. "Yes, uhm, I was told to bring my boy here by Ms. Ferby. He's not like the other children, but Ms. Ferby said she could help."

Her eyes lit up as if she was waiting for me. "Yes, dear. Ms. Ferby told me all about him, and we are so happy to have him."

She smiled and reached for my hand. I took it and let her take me into the school. I was so nervous. I thought, White people sure have been kind to me lately.

I kept lookin' back at Dre while she pulled me into the school. He hadn't ever played with other children. But he seemed alright so far. I wanted ask so badly if the other little boy in the sandbox was slow, but I kept walking.

"It ain't feeling so good leavin' my son out there without me."

"Oh, he will be fine. The other class will be out there for a break soon."

"To be honest, he ain't never played with other children, so I don't know—"

But she interrupted and said, "Ma'am, I'm sorry. What's your name?"

"Candace, ma'am," I replied.

She looked into my eyes and said, "Listen… what we do is let them be who they are. It's the only way to tell where they need to be in their growth and learning."

I looked at her like she was crazy. It just didn't make sense to me, but they were smart and knew better than I did. I looked out the screen door and Dre was just pouring sand into the tin can, smiling and clapping his hands.

"See, Ms. Candace?" the teacher said. "Some children need other children around to feel a sense of belonging."

I smiled at her and turned around toward the classroom. It was filled with books, colorful pictures on the wall, and all kinds of toys. The classroom was old and run down, with a few busted windows boarded up. The little desks were just a fit for the children. Each desk had a pencil and paper waiting for the children when they came back in the room.

"I'm sorry. I never asked your name, ma'am."

She laughs, "I never told you either, so I am sorry too. It's Lorraine."

"Ms. Lorraine, what is the child doing back there in the corner? Is she slow if you don't mind me asking?" Ms. Lorraine looked back toward the little girl and said, "Oh, that's sweet Sarah. No, she's not slow. She can't hear. She is deaf and mute."

"How can she learn if she can't hear?" I didn't know if that was a stupid question or not. But I wanted to know.

"We are teaching her to use her hands to tell us what she needs. Some call it finger spelling. She is taught to use her fingers to spell words. Let's walk back there. Sarah is six years old and is being raised by her grandmother."

"She makes sounds, but we are working with her to look at our lips, so we can teach her how to sign what we say and what she needs," she replied.

I didn't know what finger spelling was, and I was too afraid to ask.

"Ms. Candace, we want to teach Dre to sign as well with his hands, so you will be able to understand him like Sarah.

"Can you show me how you speak to Sarah?"

Just then, Sarah looked up with those big brown eyes. She looked like she could be Dre's sister. Her hair plaited so neat, which was lying on her shoulders. Ms. Lorraine bends down and looks into her face. She said in a low voice, "Bathroom." Sarah looked back at her and balled up her fist and waves it back and forth. Ms. Lorraine took Sarah's fist and put the thumb between the second and third finger while it's balled up. Ms. Lorriane looked Sarah in her eyes again and made a sign with her fingers and moved her lips. "Yes; good girl."

As I watched them my heart was at peace thinking of what they could do for Dre.

She walked Sarah to the bathroom in the back of the school. As soon as they got out of sight, I tried to ball my fist like Sarah but couldn't remember where the thumb went. Just then Ms. Lorraine walked up from behind me and said, "You learned that fast."

We both laughed a little. I felt at ease the more I talked to her.

"It's time for a break," she told the young colored girl who helped with the children. "You can walk them out to the yard, and I will clean up a bit."

I thought to myself, *I didn't think color people could be teachers, but I reckon they can now.*

The young girl said, "Yes, ma'am." On her way out she said to me, "Your boy is sweet, ma'am."

"Thank you kindly," I said to her as I look out the window and see Dre playing with the rocks by himself. He's lining them up one by one like he does at the house. The other children are playing around him. I don't feel bad they don't play with him. But Lord have mercy if one of them chillun mess with them rocks he got in a row. It will not be good.

As the children walk for a break, I look at each one of them. They are mostly boys. I never allowed myself to think too much about if Dre was normal. I reckoned he'd be like them. Bright eyes, curious, and could talk. Well, he got the bright-eyed part, and curious part, but he was keeping his words a secret. They were laughing and meddling with one another. Just like was when I was a child.

Dre seemed a little scared as the kids came out one by one. I was looking at him just in case I have to pull him off one of 'em. I walked toward the door to go on the porch, and Ms. Lorraine walked back in with Sarah.

"You okay with this so far, Ms. Candace? We keep busy here. So much to tend to, you know?"

"How does Sarah's grandmother feel about Sarah not hearing things?"

"You know…I believe love will allow you to handle just about anything. She is a praying woman, so I know where her strength comes from. She is good now, but it hasn't always been that way. However, it was something she got used to."

"I see what you do here and how you handle the children, and it makes me feel good," I told her.

Ms. Ferby was right, but I couldn't seem to let go of the fear of leaving Dre. Before I knew it, my eyes start feeling moist and warm. "I'm sorry. I don't mean to cry, but he needs me. I don't know what I will do without him."

"Oh, Ms. Candace; I know you scared. But don't you want him to learn?"

I couldn't seem to take no more. I dropped my pocketbook and just broke down, crying to Ms. Lorraine.

"He can't learn; he doesn't talk. He jumps up and down, he spits and hits. He doesn't love. He won't even look at me."

Now Ms. Lorraine looked nervous. I'm sure she was thinking *Dre's mama having a fit too.*

"Ms. Candace, please calm down," she said instead. "Sit here for a while…and here's a couple of tissues to wipe your face. You'll scare the poor children to death."

I sat down slowly and start wiping my eyes. "I don't know what happened to me. I've never said anything like that about Dre out loud. Only to myself…and when I talk to God."

Ms. Lorraine sat in the chair next to me. "Let me say this; all children are special. Some just need more attention than others. But we must love them the best way we can. They teach us how to love them in their own way. Dre loves everything about you."

"How do you know?" I was so ashamed for yelling and crying like I did. "Because he wakes up to you and he knows in his little heart that you will protect him. He goes to bed each night with your gentle touch. He listens to your voice and senses the calmness. Just because he doesn't speak doesn't mean his other senses aren't working. Your boy is smarter than you think. We don't know why they have peculiar ways, but we can't give up on them 'cause they different. We give them all we have, and with the hope that the good Lord will do the rest."

I kept thinking about how I acted at the schoolhouse today. I can't get those thoughts out of my head. Ms. Lorraine was so comforting. I never told anyone how I really felt about Dre other than May Esther, but I never showed it like I did with Ms. Lorraine. In the deepest part of my heart, God knows I love my son. I believe it will get better.

Chapter 20

School

It'd been a week since he joined school, and I 'clare Dre can't wait to go to school. On Saturdays, I must tell him "No school" a thousand times. Otherwise, he'd try to leave out the door. Then he pulls out them books. I don't mind, as long it keeps him from trying to run out the door.

He seemed to be doin' okay in school. He had one of them fits one week, but no spittin', scratching, or biting his hand. Lately, he'd go running to his room, turn to the wall, and start rockin' back and forth. I didn't know how they got him to do that. I didn't think they hit him or tie him down.

The teachers seemed to like Dre. They all say nice things about him as if he was kin. Mama felt they must be doing right by him, 'cause he was gettin' a feeling of being around humans. Sometimes, mama can say things as if Dre ain't even human. May Esther used to cry about a normal life. I don't think mine is normal at all. I really miss dreamin' with May. She would put all kinds of things in my head. She wanted to sit by the ocean and watch the sun rise and set. I would laugh at her and say, "Where you get that from, May?" She would look up to the sky and say "God," and then close her eyes, as if she was saying a prayer. I loved her way of dreamin'. She loved putting her feet in the sand on the ground. Well, it was really dirt but you couldn't tell her it wasn't sand when she daydreamed. Lord knows I missed my friend. I pray she is somewhere living her dreams.

Mama wanted us to go to church with her today. I hadn't been feeling like going 'cause Dre couldn't handle that place. Once they started singing, he got nervous and wanted to leave. I'd take him out back, so the noise wouldn't bother him. But before I'd take him out, the people kept right on clappin' and singing. It could've been to drown him out.

It was a little cool this morning, for September in the Carolinas.

"Dre, come on now, Shug, let's go to the church to see mama and papa," I told him.

I didn't think he would run through the house like he did. That meant he was ready. You would think I called him to eat sugarcane stick. I walked through the house to make sure I had my Bible and then I went upstairs to Dre's room. Dre had torn pages out of the books and made paper airplanes. They were all over the floor. I couldn't yell at him 'cause I knew he saw somebody at the schoolhouse do it. It made me smile.

Chapter 21

Confirmation

It was the day Ms. Ferby got back in town. I hadn't seen her since I took Dre to the school. She would be happy to know that he was there. She'd been up in New York City doin' testing and things so she could teach the kids. I watched the teachers at Dre's school and how they marked the schoolwork the children do. It got so, that I was just as excited for him to go to school, because he was finally learning like the other children.

Dre ran in the school as he did every morning. Before he sat at his desk, he counted the nails on the wood on top of the desk. He then walked around the desk five times before he sat down. The teacher already has the pencil and paper out for him just to keep him busy. I liked to sit in somedays and listen to the teachers teach. I hadn't sat in Dre's class though. I didn't want to make him fidgety.

Ms. Ferby walked in with her seeing stick, sliding it from side to side, making sure nothing was in her way. The wood floors had stick marks that she made every day. Her dark glasses covered her eyes completely. She'd been gone a long while. She'd cut her long stringy hair into a short cut close to her head. Must be easier to care for. Her white sweater looked like it was fresh out of the store. She looked like a new Ms. Ferby. The city must've changed her, I supposed.

"Hey, Ms. Ferby; it's Dre's mama. Candace."

"Ms. Candace, come here. It's so good to see you." She grabbed me as if she could see me right through those glasses. Ms. Ferby was so filled with life and joy. I couldn't imagine how she laughs and smiles at the children. They love her so much. "Ms. Candace, I heard nothin' but good news about Dre," she went on. "I am sure he is excited to be here. As I knew he would be. Now how do you feel about this, Ms. Candace? Please, let's sit here and talk."

I walked over to her to sat down and started fixin' my hair and straightenin' out my clothes as if she could see me. "I reckon I don't know how I feel. I think I am happy and scared at the same time."

She laughed as if I said something funny. She was tender lady, and the haircut made her look more like a child.

"Ms. Candace, I came from a home where anything is possible. Dre may not be like any of these precious children, but he is precious. Dre is a gift from God. Sometimes, a gift doesn't always come as we expect, but when we open it and see what it is…Lord have mercy…it's nothing you asked for, but you love and appreciate it because it's yours from God.

"I was speaking with some of the teachers and professors up north, and they are doing testing, trying to figure out what could be the problem with children like Dre," she added.

I gave her a frightened look and said, "Is he retarded, ma'am?"

Ms. Ferby searched for my hand and started moving her head from side to side. "No, he is not," Ms. Ferby said it with a stern voice. "I know a professor who is studying that behavior—"

"No, Ms. Ferby!" I pulled away from her hand. "They gone give my baby medicine or put wires up to his head, like he crazy. No. I won't do it. You said Dre could learn to be normal."

Ms. Ferby reached her hand toward me and said, "Ms. Candace, please listen to me. I am here to help you; the Good Lord knows I am. Please sit down and just listen to me. I used to hear my mother cry because I couldn't see like the other children. I was a happy child, and I thought I was like everyone else. The children played with me as though I could see them. When my mama and papa realized it, they started treating me as if I could see. They made the house fit for me, even though I ran around like a wild goose." Ms. Ferby started laughing at this. Then she kept going. "As I got older, my mama wanted me to learn like the other children who could see. She found out about Heller Keller. She couldn't hear or see, but she learned by finger spelling from a teacher. In which, that is what we will teach Dre."

Ms. Ferby had my full attention. "You know who told my mama about Helen Keller?" I look at her like I am about to open a surprise.

"Who?"

"Ms. Agnes. She sure did. You know Ms. Agnes was a smart woman. That's why you are smart, Ms. Candace. So many people looked up to Ms. Agnes. She was a Sunday school teacher, and she would come down to the schoolhouse and help the teachers with the children who needed special attention."

"Like Dre?"

"Yes, Ms. Candace; kids that were like me and your Dre."

I felt a tear start to fall down my cheek. While Ms. Ferby was talking, I thought about Ms. Agnes and how I missed her so much. "Ms. Agnes loved me, Ms. Ferby," I said.

"I believe it, Candace; she had a big heart. I don't think she looked at anyone's color. She loved everyone."

Ms. Agnes would have helped me with Dre. He would probably be talking now I reckoned. Ms. Ferby stretched as she pulled her chair to the side. "Come here, Ms. Candace." She put her arms around me and said, "Maybe God sent me in Ms. Agnes' place. I want to help you and Dre. I know you thinking how a White, blind teacher gonna teach Dre. But Helen Keller learned, and because she learned, I was able to."

I hugged Ms. Ferby and cried. Ms. Ferby hugged me tightly. At that moment, I felt that hug was Ms. Agnes.

Chapter 22

Mama's Feeling

"Oooh, mama, these lima beans and biscuits are so good! Mine don't turn out like these. Look at Dre; he love 'em too."

"Candace, you got to let them soak before you cook them."

"But, mama, don't it make the skin come off?"

"Yeah, mama and Aunt Lucy used to cook them that way. They cook faster too," mama said as she sat down and watched us eat like we hadn't eaten in days.

Then, mama looked at Dre and said, "Dre, Shug, don't eat with your hands. Mama got a nice spoon for you." I couldn't take it and yelled at Dre, as if to let mama know I am training him. I yelled, "Dre Anthony, don't use your hands!"

I scared him and he threw his plate across the room. Then he kicked the chair over, went moving over to the stove, and fell out on the floor. I tried to grab him before he got over to the stove. I grabbed his hands, but he tried to bite me.

"Candace, you should beat him. He knows better. He needs a good lashin'," mama said.

"No, mama; Dre has special needs. That's what the teacher says, and I have to take care of him. He will get better in time."

I didn't know what to do now that mama had seen him behave that way. I couldn't take another long talk from mama about Dre being retarded. Now that Ms. Ferby said he ain't retarded, that was what I was going to believe. I sneaked a look at mama and knew she felt bad for saying it. I took Dre by the hand and he walked with me to the door.

"Candace, I reckon he got issues, but you can't let him run over you."

"Mama, he got to control me. 'Cause I don't know what else to do with him but love him." I kissed her cheek and walked out the door. I felt bad leaving mama to clean up the mess Dre left, but if papa walked in and saw it, he may get the switch to his butt.

Ms. Ferby told me she had a friend coming to the schoolhouse one day. She thought he may be able to work with Dre on using words. I felt good about Ms. Ferby looking after me and Dre. It was the best feeling I had in a long time. I pray he will be able to help.

Ms. Ferby had her teachers working with him so much that he could sit still long enough to look through a book. Every now and then, he got up to sit in the corner. Where they kept the stack of books. The teachers thought it was better for Dre when it was quiet. They could tell when he didn't want to be around the other children. Ms. Ferby said children like Dre must be on a set schedule, so they try not to make him do new things too often that may upset him. They even taught him how to shake his thumb when he has to go to the bathroom, like the little deaf girl Sarah in his class. I was so happy that he could learn that. I still didn't understand how they got Sarah to speak by finger spelling.

I was lying in bed thinking about all that God has done for me and Dre. I still don't know what all of this means. I find myself afraid to ask questions. Growing up, I used to think what life would be like for me and mama and papa. I didn't know what mama thought about me having Dre. I never forgot what she said when I told her that I was with child.

She said, "Oh no, Candace, Lord have mercy!" I never thought she would be happy about it, and I was afraid she would be so embarrassed that she would tell me to give it away. I never once thought in my mind that I would do that anyway. Yes, I was scared, but I knew I had a real life inside me, and it was from God. It's like what Ms. Agnes would say about joy. She would say, "Joy is something you feel on the inside, which no man can take from you. It makes you happy, Candace. Always remember this is what the Holy Bible says…. The joy of the Lord is your strength.[1]"

---

1 *The Bible, "Do not grieve, for the joy of the Lord is your strength" Nehemiah 8:10*

Chapter 23

How Sweet the Touch

Well, it was time. Mr. Anderson, the professor from New York, was comin' to see about Dre. Ms. Ferby came to the house the previous day to see if I'd changed my mind.

"Ms. Candace, how you been doing?" she asked.

I was always staring at her because I couldn't believe she got around so good. She is truly a special gift from God.

"I am doing fine, ma'am, just finished supper. I can fix you a plate, ma'am, if you hungry."

Ms. Ferby laughed. "No thank you, but it sure smells good." Dre had become so fond of Ms. Ferby, when he sees her, he runs up to her and plays with her hands. I guess it's from what he was learning in school, finger spelling. She was so good with Dre.

We could hear him running back and forth upstairs, playing. I went to the bottom of the steps and called him, "Dre, come here, baby; Ms. Ferby is here to see you."

He ran down the steps as fast as a fox. He got to the last step and fell. Ms. Ferby stood up from her chair, concerned about his fall.

"Ms. Candace, is he okay?"

"Yes, ma'am; he does it all the time. I am used to it. He is just a tough little boy," I replied with a laugh. Dre went to Ms. Ferby and started to play with her hands. She started laughing as if it tickles her. I walked to the stove and got Dre supper. I couldn't help but look at what they were doing. She was pulling Dre's fingers apart and he was looking in her face.

She whispered "Hello" to him as she moved his fingers around. With his hands, Dre followed what Ms. Ferby was doing.

"Ma'am, do you think he is catching on to the finger spelling." I asked.

Ms. Ferby looked up to the ceiling and whispered, "Yes, yes, he is. Dre likes the movement he feels when uses his hands. It's a sense of peace I believe." Dre moved her hands to touch his head. She then whispered "head." He never spoke a word of course, he just moved his hands. She then told me to sit down, put my hands on my lap, and open them up. "Now put Dre's hands facing up on top of your hands," she said.

He looked at me, then looked away, and started humming, rubbing my face with both hands. "Now say 'face' in a low voice." I was so nervous, but I whispered "face" to him with tears rolling down my face. That touch felt like heaven. Ms. Ferby noticed the silence and she smiled. I believe she knew I was crying.

"Do you see what he is learning? He is learning words with his hands by touching and using finger movements. I whisper to him when I talk because I don't want to scare him. He reacts to noise that he is not expecting. The more I talk to him and show him what I am saying by touching parts of the body—the face, fingers, head, nose, eyes, arms, and feet. He will remember by watching this, Ms. Candace." As soon as Ms. Ferby finished talking, Dre went over to her and touched her face and head repeatedly. "You, see? This is what your boy can do. He has a remarkable memory. At the school, he looks at the board on the wall that has the ABC chart. It's also filled with numbers and pictures the teachers put together." Just from Ms. Ferby mentioning ABCs, Dre grabs her one hand and started moving her fingers. "You see, Ms. Candace? He is signing the alphabets." Ms. Ferby had pure excitement in her voice. "Pretty soon, he will know the whole alphabet like the rest of the children."

It didn't take long for Dre to eat and go upstairs to them books. "Ms. Ferby, it's getting late. I need to start cleaning up a bit. You said tomorrow is the big day."

Ms. Ferby laughed as I help her to the door and says, "Yes, God willing. God willing." That stick of hers led her outside to the top of the steps. I found myself walking with her, so she doesn't fall. She got around better than I could. "I reckon I stop by and say hello to Ms. Pearl. I know she will be happy to hear the good news about Dre progress."

Chapter 24

~

Mr. Anderson

Ms. Ferby called me over to her when she heard my voice and said, "Mr. Anderson, this is Candace."

I was too nervous to look up until he reached for my hand. When I looked at him, I couldn't help but stare, like I saw a ghost. I felt faint. He squeezed my hand so tight I had to pull away. I was embarrassed about my reaction. Ms. Ferby moved to the front of the classroom so we could talk in private about Dre.

"It's a pleasure to meet you, Ms. Candace. Your boy here is mighty handsome."

I knew he felt how uncomfortable I am. "Thank you, Sir. I suspect you done heard a lot about him." Dre was playing with a piece a paper he'd found on the floor. He looked up at Mr. Anderson like he was trying to remember his face, and then he ran outside to play in the sand box. I turned to look in the classroom after Dre goes out to the school yard with the children and teachers. "Yes, I have heard all good things about Dre." I was still too embarrassed to look at his face.

I could see Ms. Ferby sitting in the front of the class. She was talking to the children about the sun, moon, the sky, and rainbows. She told them God sends us rainbows to let us know He hears our prayers. The children were a little older in this class, and they were quiet as a mouse as she talked. Mr. Anderson sat down where I was standing and started unpacking his bag. "She is an amazing woman," he said, referring to Ms. Ferby. I smiled as if I was looking at her, but I am still in shock that Mr. Anderson is colored. He is a colored man from up north. I couldn't believe it. A colored man here to teach my boy how to talk. I was sure he would be White. Ms. Ferby never said a word about it. Some people don't care about color if it means to help children. I wondered why she never said anything; well, I ain't ask either.

"We can sit in the next classroom while the children have playtime," he said.

I followed behind him, and he pulled the door for me to walk through first. I looked out to see if Dre was alright. Mr. Anderson saw me watching Dre, and he laughed and said, "It's their favorite thing to do, laughing and playing in dirt."

I tried to talk a little so he wouldn't think something was wrong with me. "It's a little cold out today for August. Fall will soon be here."

Mr. Anderson was still looking through his brown bag filled with papers and books. "Well, it feels great to me. Being from New York City, I enjoy weather like this."

I paid attention to the way he talks. It was so proper and uppity. That's what we in the south called colored people from up north. I asked him to repeat himself so I could understand him.

The small talk that we had was making me feel more at ease. I hope he didn't catch me staring at him. I sat across from him like a child.

"Ms. Candace, I know you are nervous, and it's okay. This is new to you, and I understand. I heard all about Dre and the certain behaviors he has. I wanted to talk to you and tell you a bit about how we think we can help Dre in his process of learning. I have a few questions here that I want to ask you about Dre's home life and surroundings. Is that alright?"

"Yes, that will be fine."

Mr. Anderson had been back and forth to New York and Jacksonville since I met him to discuss Dre. It has been so nice to see how much attention Dre was getting, and it was making a difference. I was glad about it.

I'm so tired today. I picked Dre up from school, and we were both draggin' up the road. I didn't know who was sitting on my steps. He looks like one of my uncles friends. Lord knows I hope it's not him.

He probably had been drinking all day. I would surely know if his face was beet red. He loved Dre and stopped by sometimes to give him candy. I was getting closer, and I 'clare that looked Mr. Anderson sitting on my steps. It was nice out this afternoon; maybe he wanted to take a walk. Ms. Ferby must have told him where my house was. I wasn't expecting him. *Now what in the world could be wrong?* I wondered.

"Dre, I get to see you twice today."

Dre took off running to him. He reached for Dre's hand to shake it, and Dre slapped it and ran to the door. "I'm sorry for that slap, Mr. Anderson."

"That's okay. He is acknowledging my presence," he laughs.

"Is everything okay, Mr. Anderson? I wasn't expecting to you today, unless Ms. Ferby told me, and I forgot."

He stepped down off the steps and shook my hand. "No, no; I came on my own. I left the schoolhouse before you arrived with Dre this morning. I hope you don't mind. Ms. Ferby said you didn't have a telephone, and I had no way of contacting you. So, she gave me the address. I was going to ask if I could stop by your house to work with Dre." He was just a-talking, and I was thinking about what May Esther said about men she would see. She would tell me stories about she met a "pure pretty man." I would ask her "What you mean by a pretty man?" She'd say he would have smooth skin, a nice mustache, clean haircut. I know when I was younger my Aunt Lily Mae and Aunt Bertha Mae would say a good-looking man looked like a "Piece of lemon meringue pie," and it would tickle me so much. They would say that for sure about Mr. Anderson.

I stared at Mr. Anderson like he a pretty man. I couldn't see him as a piece of pie though. "I'm sorry. I don't have nothing to offer but sweet tea. I haven't started supper yet."

"No, I'm fine; thank you. I wanted to talk to you for a few minutes about the papers we went over about Dre at the school the other day. A few of the professors up north are studying different types of children's behavior as I told before."

Of course, I was uneasy when he says that, but I listened.

"To be honest, I don't know what you going to study about Dre, Mr. Anderson. He doesn't talk, but Ms. Ferby say he is learning really good, and his memory is the best for a child." It seemed like them doctors up north got so much to study when it comes to Dre. I wondered what they gonna say.

Mr. Anderson said, "What you mean is Dre can't speak, and he has peculiar ways. There are a lot of children in the world who behave like Dre."

"Mr. Anderson, some folk call kids like him dumb or retarded. It's a woman at the warehouse where I work, her boy at St. Elizabeth hospital. They call him a mongoloid. I don't want that for Dre. I would hide him 'fore I let anyone take him away."

"I understand. Ms. Ferby told me about your concerns. You are right; he does not belong in the hospital. What I observed from him so far is quite remarkable. Dre is listening, even when you don't know he is listening. The finger spelling he has learned has impressed me and Ms. Ferby, as well as yourself, I'm sure. The way he loves books, and his eagerness to learn new things… he's smarter than most of the kids in his age group.

"The study is to see if there are other ways to care for the hundreds of children like him. For example, Ms. Ferby has one of the teachers sit with Dre and observe him when comes to school. He likes routine. He likes to do the same things repeatedly. He never likes to go out of the patterns he has. Due to this, it takes a while for him to get settled at his desk, even during lunch and I assume dinner. Do you understand what I mean, Ms. Candace?"

"I reckon I don't really."

"Ms. Candace, look at me." He grabbed my hand slowly. "I know this is a lot, but I believe by the Grace of God, Dre is going to do great things. I am willing to see to it, and Ms. Ferby. The Lord didn't send me here to hurt, but to help."

Mr. Anderson took off his suit jacket and laid it on the steps. I was so sad, but it didn't come from what he what saying about Dre. I was upset that I didn't understand most of what he what saying. I didn't want him to know that.

"I want to give you a hug and let you know that I am proud of you, for allowing us to help Dre. You don't mind do you, Ms. Candace?"

I laughed a little and said, "No, sir, it's okay." It felt nice to feel cared for.

"Please try to see this whole process as hope for Dre, Ms. Candace," he added.

I stepped away from his arms. The hug was what I needed. I felt safe and cared about. It was only a minute, but it felt like forever, like wakin' up from a dream. I wiped my eyes, and he handed me his handkerchief. "No, no, I don't want to get it dirty," I said. He laughed and said, "I have more."

"This is all scary and comforting at the same time. I can't thank you and Ms. Ferby enough for wanting to help us. I feel like God sent His angels. I better get in here and check on Dre and get supper started."

He put his suit jacket on and said, "It was a pleasure. I'm sorry I didn't get to do much with Dre tonight. Do you think it will be alright to come back tomorrow and do what I started out to do today?" Before I could think about it, my mouth said that it will be fine.

"Do you think you might want to stay for supper? I expect you tired of the food in town. I understand if you can't." I was just talking so much, like somebody pushed a button on my throat.

"I sure would like that Ms. Candace, very much. That is so kind of you, thank you. Have a good evening." Dre came outside as I watched Mr. Anderson walk away. I grabbed his hand. "Mama gonna give you a piece of jelly cake before supper." He looked at his hand and I reckoned that meant yes. I whisper a prayer: *Give me hope, Father God…I know that all other ground is sinking sand.*

Chapter 25

Mama

"Mama, I can always smell your cooking before I get to your house. One day, I'm gonna be able to cook like you. I think after tending to Ms. Agnes all of them years I done lost the soul in my cooking," I said and laughed as we sat around mama's kitchen table.

"Candace, you look good, shug. Since you been working, I don't get to see you and Dre as much."

"Mama, it's only been two weeks or so."

"Well, I miss Dre and his Granddaddy does too. He said Dre needed a haircut last time he saw him."

"How is papa doin', mama?"

"You know he has his good and bad days. He can't shake that cough he has, but it doesn't stop him from being out on that farm all day with your uncles." mama then sat and looked at me like she worried. "Is everything okay with you and Dre, baby? Do you need food or money?"

"No, ma'am, we do alright with the money I make at the warehouse. It's been two months now, and they haven't let me go yet. It's easier working while Dre is in school. Thank the Good Lord." And then I added, "Mama, Dre doing so good in school! He loves it and Ms. Ferby and the teachers done taught him so much. He is learning how to talk with his hands and makes letters and numbers with his fingers. They call it finger spelling." I knew this would be the beginning of a thousand questions.

"How you do speak with your hands, Candace?"

I already see the doubt in mama's eyes.

"It's a certain language they have for people who can't hear. Dre can hear but he can't talk, so this gets him to communicate."

Mama sat down and wiped her hands on her apron and looked at the wall as if she saw a ghost. I have all of her attention now. "He is so smart, mama. He knows how to show you the alphabet with his fingers."

"I don't understand all this mess. I thought they would get him to talk. What happened? It doesn't make sense to me." mama always thought Dre was retarded, and I know it is hard for her to understand, but he isn't retarded. I wish she would be more caring. I try to change the subject and talk about Mr. Anderson. I know this will confuse her even more after I tell her all about him.

"I met the Professor from New York Ms. Ferby has been talking about."

Mama walks over to the window. This a lot for her because she worries so much.

"Oh yeah. I reckoned he the one that made up all this talking with your hands?"

"Mama, this is new to me too. You told me to take Dre to the school and I did. I was scared and I still am, but I see what he is learning, and it makes me feel good. Ms. Ferby can't see a thing, and she is helping me like we kin. Mr. Anderson came all the way from New York to study Dre and his ways. He ain't said nothing about no medicine for Dre at all. Guess what else?" mama turned around after she heard me sniffling and crying a little. "Mama, Mr. Anderson is colored and really cares. He said there are children all over the world like Dre. He works with Dre when he comes in town."

"Hush yo mouth, Candace!" mama is excited now and giggling a little. "The whole time you are talking, I'm thinking for sure he a White man. So, he been by the house?"

"Yes, ma'am; he showed up yesterday and asked if he could come back again today and watch Dre's behavior. I asked if he wanted to stay for supper." I look away fast as I could so mama wouldn't try settin' up a wedding for us in her mind.

"So what he look like?" she asks.

I hesitate. "He looks like a teacher, mama." I hated I said that.

"Now what in the world does that mean?"

"I reckon he look okay. He is mighty nice, and he knows how to handle Dre."

"What you gonna fix for supper when he comes back?"

"I don't know…maybe collards, fried corn, fried chicken, and biscuits."

"I got fresh collards from the garden. You can have those. Now, how is your fried chicken? I don't think I ever tasted your chicken, Candace."

"Mama, I can cook. I don't cook like you but I can cook. I cooked for Ms. Agnes for years."

"Oh shoot; Ms. Agnes would eat anything you give her." Sometimes, mama got a sense of humor. I liked it better when she was not so stiff.

"Oh! Before I forget, that gal May Esther called here for you."

Before I knew what was happening, I threw the empty plate down to the table, ran over to mama, and hugged her. I didn't know what to say. I just hugged her. "Mama, what did she say? Is she alright? Is she here?" I never gave mama a chance to answer before I asked another question.

"She said to tell you she was doing okay, and she would write to you soon."

"I'm sorry I messed up the table. I've been worried about her since she left. She was such a good friend to me and loved Dre. I feel so good that she is fine. Thank the Lord. Did she say where she was living?"

Mama shook her head. "No, I didn't ask her. That gal was bad news. People knew what she was doing."

"Oh, mama, Nicky is long gone, and she free from him and his foolish ways." I realized it was getting late. "I have to leave, mama. I am just a wreck with Mr. Anderson coming over, but I'm happy knowing that May Esther is fine."

"It's okay, Shug. Well, you better go on now. Take them collards and wash them real good. They fresh out the garden, may have them little worms on 'em. I meant to ask you, did that teacher ask you where you got that big house from you living in?"

"No, and I don't think he will pry about it."

"Now you be careful with that teacher. You don't let everybody in your bosom. You never know, with him being from up north and all. Pray all will be well. Me and your papa will be praying too."

I hugged mama so tight and she didn't want to let me go.

She yelled out the door watching me leave like she always does, "Pray, Candace."

I rushed home to see if I got a letter from May Esther. Shucks, nothing had come. *Maybe tomorrow. Lord, I thank you that she is alright. I pray she is. Wait until she hears the good news about Dre. She always wanted more for us too*, I thought.

I tried to make things look good in the house. I got a feeling Mr. Anderson would want to look around the house. Well its all cleaned up now. It takes a while to get Dre settled. He gotta repeat things a thousand times before he moved on to the next thing. He runs to his room and takes out all the books under his bed. Then he touches each one and puts it back in its place. Some nights, he opened a book and started making finger signs, as if he knows what the words mean when he signs. I still couldn't believe he could do all of this. I smiled 'cause he's mine, and he is special. "Dre, I'm going downstairs to start supper. Mr. Anderson is coming to see you, Shug."

He ran through the front door. I got downstairs in enough time to catch him on the porch, then he ran back in. I put the latch on the door, which he breaks at least once a week.

"Dre, where you at? Come see mama, Shug."

I found him in the corner playin with something. I didn't expect response when I mentioned Mr. Anderson's name. Maybe he will stay busy until I finish supper.

Everything looked good, I guess. The house was smelling right nice. I don't think I could sweep this floor anymore. I'd been over it at least five times. Lord! That is him already.

"Ms. Candace, it's me, Mr. Anderson."

I snatched my apron off and throw it on the chair. "Hey there, come on in, sir. Supper is just about done. Please have a seat."

"My, my! This is a fine house you have here. It's as big as the school house."

We both laughed, but mine was a nervous laugh. "Dre, Mr. Anderson is here."

I called him about three times, and he still doesn't come. I was thinking Mr. Anderson would see Dre go into one of his fits. "I will be right back. Please have a seat."

"Are you sure everything is okay?"

"Yes, he is somewhere being busy."

"If you don't mind, I'd like to look at the books you have here on this huge bookcase."

"Sure, help yourself."

When I finally found Dre, he was in my closet playing with my shoestrings. "Come on, baby, let's go see Mr. Anderson." He stood up and grabbed my hand. I washed his hands and face off before we went downstairs. I looked at Dre and whispered, "Please, no fits, baby. Be a good boy for me and Mr. Anderson." I tried to look him in the face as if he will respond back. But I remembered what Ms. Ferby said—that I must remember the finger spelling as well. After I wiped his face, I held his arms to keep him still and said "Okay" with my mouth. He grabbed my lips and pushed away from me. I know this would take time.

"Mr. Anderson, I'm sorry it took so long. I had to get him settled for supper." Mr. Anderson looked up from a book he was flipping through. "Where was he? What was he doing?" I was nervous about answering him.

"He has these things he does every day. He likes to hide in the closet and under the steps. He finds something like a string or anything little and plays with it. Or he grabs a book and looks through it." Just then, Dre came over and sat on the floor by the steps. Mr. Anderson walked over to him and said, "Hey, smart boy." He reached down to shake Dre's hand and Dre smacked it away. Then he started playing with his fingers, with Mr. Anderson just watching him. "He just signed 'smart boy.'"

"Are you sure, Mr. Anderson?"

He laughed at me and said, "Yes, I'm sure."

I really hope that one day I will I be able to know that difference.

"He is catching on faster than we thought, Ms. Candace. Ms. Ferby is not surprised with the good reports from the teachers. Do you mind if I sit in the parlor? I need to look at a few things in this heavy bag. I think this will help me understand Dre a little better at home."

I gave him a shrug. "He doesn't do much round here but the same things. I already know what he gonna do each day here in the house."

Mr. Anderson nodded. "The key with children like Dre is they like to do the same things repeatedly. It's called repetition. It gives them sense of comfort. What you and I find comfort in is different. What you don't realize, Ms. Candace, is that you have adapted to Dre's ways."

I sat down in the chair, so I could focus on understanding him. "Your day is routine too. You try to control Dre's outbursts by keeping him comfortable, by doing what he wants to do. I believe that one day children like Dre will be able to live a normal life."

I leaned forward and looked him in the eye and said, "My child is normal!" Just then I wanted to tell him to leave my house, but I gathered myself and calmed down.

"I mean no harm by what I said Ms. Candace. Dre is not like the other children at the school because he can't communicate with speech. I am here to help you. Trust is a hard thing when you don't have hope. I want you to help us help you, Ms. Candace."

"I know, but the word 'normal' always scares me and it still does. I wake up with hope and move about my life as if it's easy, but it ain't. The easy part is opening my eyes, and that Dre is showing signs of change for the better."

"Dre goes to school, and Ms. Ferby and the other teachers are willing to do what it takes to make changes." Sometimes he talked just like May Esther. He said things to make me listen.

I trusted him, I guess, but I was too shamed to tell him that. I walked back and forth across the floor while he was talking. I was listening to every word even though I didn't understand it all.

Dre heard him talking and walked over. He sat at Mr. Anderson's feet with a book from the shelf. He never looked up at Mr. Anderson. He was just sittin' there. The whole time Mr. Anderson been talking, Dre was sitting in the corner with that book, and then he got up and sat at his feet. "Hey there, smart boy. What you got there?" Mr. Anderson asked. Dre never looked at anyone no longer than a second. I get to look into his beautiful eyes when he is staring at things. He never looked me in my face. Mr. Anderson looked at Dre and smiled. "This is the kind of thing I need to see while I'm here. Hey, smart boy." He calls him a smart boy again. This time, Dre looked up and moved his fingers around. Mr. Anderson said with excitement in his voice, "He signed 'smart boy' again!" He laughed and reached down to Dre's hand. Just like before, Dre slapped it and kept turning the pages of the book. Mr. Anderson wrote a few things on the paper he has.

"I will leave you two alone so I can set up for supper," I said.

He didn't answer me; he just kept writing. A few minutes later, I popped my head in the room, wonderin' what they were doing 'cause they were so quiet. My mind drifted off into a daydream. I thought to myself: *This is the first time in a long-time silence didn't make me sad.*

Chapter 26

~

May Esther

I walked to mama's house to see papa after I picked up Dre. "Hey, papa! Don't get to see you much lately."

Papa look tired, but nothing could keep him from that farm. "Well, looka here. Mama told me you came by the other evenin'. My, my, my! Look at how big that boy got. Shake my hand, little fellow." He slapped papa's hand like he does Mr. Anderson. Papa always looked at him with this proud look on his face every time he sees him. Already, Dre had found something to play with on the floor. Papa sat down at the table, rubbin' his knees. I believe he was in pain but he didn't want you to make a fuss over him, so he wouldn't say.

"Where is mama, papa?"

"She down there at the church house."

«papa, I got so much to tell you about Mr. Anderson, if mama haven't told you."

"Well, you know your mama. She so busy worrying that she can't even talk about it. She mentioned some things to me. Now, who is this Anderson fella? I don't know of no Andersons from around these parts."

"He is a teacher—well, professor—from New York. He's here working at the school with Dre and other children. Dre is learning so much, papa. They are teaching him how to use his fingers and hands to communicate since he doesn't talk. They call it finger spelling if mama didn't tell you."

Papa looking at me strange.

"That's a little odd to me and your mama, Shug. He ain't asking for no money, is he?"

"No, sir; they ain't asking for nothing. They want to help children. He knows about children like Dre. He said their chillun all over the world that act like him, and some worse than others Papa, Dre is so smart. He has learned so much since they been teaching him. I never thought he would be doing any of this, and I thank the Good Lord."

Papa was watching Dre move around on the floor. "I 'clare he seems more settled in his ways. Does he have those spells he was havin'?"

"Haven't had one in a while now."

"They ain't slippin' him no medicine, are they?"

"No, sir. Ms. Ferby and Mr. Anderson said soon Dre gone learn how to read and use the finger spelling at the same time. He already learned the ABCs." Explaining things to papa was easier than saying them to mama. "The teachers say he real smart and he learn fast. They don't teach him with the other kids. They sit him in corner, so the noise won't scare him too much." I looked around mama's kitchen. It was so nice and clean. Everything in its place. "papa, you know the folks round here thinks Dre is retarded. I know mama does too, but he not. They gonna have a name for what he got soon."

"Does that White man know what he talking about? And I mean no harm by saying this, but do that blind teacher know what she talking 'bout too? You know some of them want to figure out what's wrong with colored folk."

«papa, mama didn't tell you Mr. Anderson is colored?"

Papa had this surprised look on his face when I asked that. The wrinkles on his forehead got deeper.

"You know your mama can go on and on when she starts talking. Never said a word. Say it ain't so!" We both laughed

"Yes, sir, I am shocked she didn't tell you," I said. "papa, he came over to the house to see how Dre acts at home a few times. I even had him for supper."

"Where is he living at? Does he have family here?"

"No, sir, he just came to Jacksonville to help Ms. Ferby with Dre and other children." I could tell papa had so many questions but he didn't know what to ask first. I knew he didn't understand it all. I started picking the field peas mama left soaking in the bucket. The phone rang, and papa got up to answer. I was glad, 'cause it gave me a chance to take a break from explainin'. I heard papa say mama wasn't home and asked who it was. When he said, "May who?"

I screamed as loud as I could. "May Esther! Wait, papa she wants to reach me!" papa reached out and gave me the phone.

"May, is it you? I screamed excitedly into the phone. "Oh Lord! May, is it really you? It's Candace!" She was so happy to hear from me. "May, where are you?" I asked. "Are you okay? I got so much to tell you, I 'clare I do. Dre and I miss you so much. You in Georgia?" I'd been so worried about May Esther. I didn't let myself think about what could have happened to her. We laughed a little, and she was in tears hearing about Dre. She told me she'd be here on Sunday morning. "God bless you, May…I'm glad you alright." I put the phone down and cried, holding my heart.

"What you crying for, Candy?" papa didn't know much about May Esther. He heard all the gossip, but papa wasn't a gossiping man. I never heard him say a bad thing about anybody. He would say, "We will pray for them." Folk would say, "Your papa is a good Christian." mama would say it too. "May had to leave town, papa, and I was worried about her safety. I can't wait to sit on the porch like old times and laugh, dream, and hope."

"So, I want hear more about this Anderson person." papa didn't have much of an education, but he was smart. Especially in math. The White farmers would trust papa to add up the numbers for them.

«papa, Ms. Ferby had sent for him to come and help with children like Dre," I explained. Dre don't think like most children his age. They said Dre's brain focus on the same thing repeatedly. He doesn't play with other children at school. It is a little deaf girl in the same class too. Dre walks in the school some days and goes right to his desk, or he sits on the floor and turns the pages on the books. He likes to stare at the ABC board they have on the wall right by his desk. The teachers seem to think that even though doesn't talk, he is listening. He got a long way to go, papa, but there is hope."

"I reckon that's good. We ain't never stopped praying for what The Almighty can do. Do you know how to do that thing with your fingers or hands?"

I smile and say, "Just a little. I know how to say go to the bathroom." papa laughed and said, "That's important."

"You know, I didn't know what to do about Dre not talking. I was scared and I didn't want anybody to know. I would think to myself that Dre would always be an idiot. Mama would say she thinks he is retarded, and I would go home and cry my eyes out. I would not come out the house for days, 'cause I didn't want no one to know and try to take him from me. I found myself asking God why He didn't let him talk."

"Now, ain't no way me or your mama would let that happen. Nobody would ever take him. I didn't know your heart was so troubled, Shug," papa said.

I didn't worry papa too much, so I changed the subject. I sat on the floor next to Dre. "papa, you believe in spirits?"

"You mean from dead folk?"

"Yes, sir."

"Uhh, I never thought about it. Dead folk don't bother me. I won't hear them no way with my old age hearing."

«papa, I think sometimes that Ms. Agnes' spirit is in that house. When I lay down at night, I hear a humming sound. That's all she used to do around the house."

"I wouldn't fret about the noise too much. That's an old house, and the wood floor could be rot in some places, and the windows whistlin'. It could be anything causing that noise."

"I reckon you right. Oh, that bucket in the attic is full of water from the leak on the roof. Do you think you can empty it for me? It's gotten too heavy for me."

"I will try to get up there in the morning. I will get your Uncle Doug to help. With these knees of mine."

"Come on, Dre; let's get on up the road. Papa, you need me to do anything for you before I leave?" papa was sitting back in the chair lookin' at Dre, as if he was praying for him. He never made me feel like he was ashamed of Dre. I knew mama was ashamed of him. I wanted papa to hold me and tell me it's gonna get better. It's because mama just don't understand. I miss Ms. Agnes so much. I looked for her to make sense of things. "Candy, your mama ain't never been the type to act like she cares, but she do. She right proud of you and scared for you. Your mama can't fix it and it scares her. Don't go on away from here feeling sorry for yourself."

"I won't, papa. Tell mama we came by. I will be back before Sunday. Dre still needs a haircut."

"If you need anything, come see me and your mama. That's what we here for. And remember now: He can do anything! He is the Almighty! You keep praying and don't you ever give up hope." Then, papa bent down to Dre and said, "You be a good boy, you hear?"

«papa he just signed 'good boy. I think'"

"He did?"

"Yes, I believe so."

"Ain't that something. You can talk to people without saying a word. Now, that is the work of The Almighty."

Chapter 27

The Outing

Mr. Anderson had been over to the house a quite a few times. Dre is comfortable with him more than ever. He knew how to talk to Dre, and Dre was just a-clinging to him every time he saw him. He liked to sit by his feet when he came to the house.

"Mr. Anderson, do you think might want supper?"

"I was thinking, Ms. Candace, since you been so kind and hospitable, that maybe I can take you and Dre to supper at the diner in town?"

I'd never took Dre into town before, especially to a diner. I was always afraid that the noise and crowds would send him into a fit. I started thinking what it would be like to be out with Mr. Anderson too. If May Esther was here, she would sho' 'nuff tease me and tell me I'm courtin'.

"I don't know how I feel about that."

"Is there a problem, Ms. Candace?"

I was ashamed to say it. "Well, I never took Dre so much as around a crowd other than the church house. But never into town with me. I always thought he would have them fits around crowds."

He laughed and stared at me, and said, "I will be with you, and it will be fine."

Now, I really didn't know what to say. The way he looked at me was different. Dre's father never looked at me that way. I said slowly, "I reckon that will be okay."

He was so happy, and I was so scared. "Good. I will help Dre put his blocks in the box while you get ready. Take your time." I never thought about going into town much. I don't think about going anywhere nice. The people that know me would be staring and gossiping. It didn't matter to me though. My baby was getting the help he needed, and that was all my heart cared about.

"I'm ready, Mr. Anderson." I didn't want to sound too excited, but I was. "Ms. Candace, you should try getting outdoors more. Not just taking Dre back and forth to school or going to work. Sometimes, you must look around and appreciate the trees, green grass, the moon, and the stars. You know what they say up north? That the sunlight can change a bad mood into a good mood. You know it will uplift your spirits"

"Is that right?" Dre was enjoying being outside, walking and playing with Mr. Anderson's key rope. "I'm surprised he hasn't tried to run away from you yet. That's why I'm nervous."

"I have his hand tight enough, so he feels comfortable." There was something about Mr. Anderson that made Dre feel that way. They were just walking and Mr. Anderson was talking and signing to Dre. Mr. Anderson would say, "Look, Dre, there is a dog," and he will sign it to him. "There is a cat, a car, a bus."

"You know, Mr. Anderson, as crazy as it may sound, it's okay if he doesn't talk. I see that he is learning. It may not be like the other chillun learn, but at least he learnin'."

"Ms. Candace, you reached a level that most families don't reach. Ms. Ferby would tell me about Dre and you as well. She would tell me there is a young colored boy that doesn't talk and have the same behaviors as the some of the children in the schools up north. The teachers who assist her would monitor Dre for her, and tell her how he responds to different tasks, or even if he responds at all. They were her eyes so to speak. She was so sure that Dre could be helped." The whole time Mr. Anderson was talking, I was thinking, *I sho' do need to thank Ms. Pearl. I thought that nosey woman was tryin' to put Dre in St. Elizabeth.*

"When I met Ms. Ferby and saw she was blind, I thought 'how can she know what is best for Dre?' I didn't know what to think," I said.

"You'd be surprised what people like Ms. Ferby can do."

"I see for myself now. My mama kept trying to convince me that she could teach Dre to talk. I know mama is disappointed that he still can't talk. It's hard for old folk to understand a new way of doing things."

"Ms. Candace, this is the beginning of a new way. Look at him. He hasn't tried to run away at all. He is looking around and playing with my key rope and doesn't have a care in the world. I know he feels safe. You must let Dre know that he is safe. To be honest, you must make every child feel safe. However, the everyday noise doesn't make him feel safe. He doesn't know what to expect or know how to communicate the feeling of being afraid yet."

"Mr. Anderson, I can't thank you enough for this today. I haven't felt this good in a long time."

He stopped suddenly and said, "My name is Thomas, and I want you to call me that from now on."

The way he stared at me. It was that feeling again. May Esther told me as if she was sure of it, "One day, you will get a feeling and you won't know what to do with it." She said that was the feeling she was searching for. This has got to be the feeling, and she was right about it. "Okay, Thomas." I laughed. "Well, I reckon it's time for you to stop calling me Ms. Candace."

He laughed and looked down at Dre and smiled.

Downtown Jacksonville was so pretty. A town full of marines living on the Camp Lejeune base. It made me think of Dre's daddy. I often wondered if he looks for me. Maybe not. He spoke of seeing the world, just like May Esther did. Soon I realized I'd just got lost in my past when I had my future in front of me.

"Okay, Mr. Dre, let's go in and eat. After you, Candace," he said as he held the door for me. I felt so shy but cared for even if it was just for this moment.

Chapter 28

~

A Testimony

May Esther decided to come home on Monday instead of the previous day. I cleaned up and swept all through the house. I sure hope she will be here for a while. I had so much to tell her I didn't know where to start. It has been so easy getting Dre to school. He rushes me. If he could talk, he would probably call me a slowpoke. Thomas was gone for a few days, and I missed him, I reckon. One thing I could tell May was that I was happy. I'd been smilin' more, and I found myself laughing over nothing. My baby got a long road ahead of him, but I will never give up on him. Ms. Agnes' favorite hymn was The Lord Will Provide. I could honestly say the Lord was doing just that.

It was afternoon; May had said it'll be close to two before she arrived. Maybe she'd walk with me to pick up Dre. I wondered if he will remember her. After all, he did feel safe around May Esther too. He loved when she read to him.

"Candace!"

"Lord, May, is that you? May!" I grabbed her, and we held each other and cried.

"Candace, I missed you so much. I haven't met anyone as sweet as you," she said.

"Oh, hush your mouth, May Esther. Step back; let me see you."

May Esther was looking like a new woman. She looked so pretty and healthy. She got a new fancy hairdo. "May Esther, I 'clare, you look good. It does my heart some kind of good to see you smiling. I was so worried about you after you slipped away from here. I still have the letter you left me."

She grabbed her bag and walked into the kitchen. We used to start our talks in there and end up on the front porch, no matter what the weather was like. We'd be out there late into the night after I put Dre to sleep and Nicky was out of town.

"So…" We said it the same time and burst into laughter. "Okay, May, you go first." May was talking so fast, just like old times, and I got every word. She talked just like a teacher.

"When I left Nicky, I met a man who lived in Georgia. He was the last man I met when I left Nicky. He said he was going back to Georgia, and I asked him if I could go back with him. When I got there, I didn't have a place to stay, so he let me stay there until I got a job. After a week, he talked to someone he knew who worked at the hospital, and I got a job as a telephone operator. He helped me out a lot. He is an incredibly good man.

"And guess what else, Candace?"

"What, gal?" I said with excitement.

"I went to school, and I got my nursing certificate. I'm a nurse, Candace! Can you believe it?"

"May, that's what you always wanted to be." I hugged her with so much joy in my heart. "A nurse! Lord have mercy; the Lord is so good."

"Yes, He is, Candace, and I go to church now, every Sunday including prayer meeting. Can you believe it? I moved out of his house when I made enough money. I really wasn't ready to live with another man. I want to take care of myself, for once in my life. And I want to help people."

May got up and looked toward the clouds. "I think about those old times almost every day, Candace. Even though I didn't know if I could ever leave Nicky, I never thought it would ever happen. So, where is Dre now?"

I looked at her right proud and said, "School."

"Lord Jesus, Candace, say it ain't so!"

"Yes, it is so. May, so much has happened. I finally decided to take Dre to the schoolhouse. It's been a year since he started. You know, ever since I found you and Dre in the attic when you were hiding from Nicky, it made me think about him loving the books so much. He still has his peculiar ways, but May, he is so smart. They have a blind teacher, Ms. Ferby, who believed she could help. They also have a deaf child in the classroom with Dre. She knows how to use her fingers for words, called finger spelling, to say what she feels and communicate."

"Yes, yes, I know all about that. I see a few patients in the hospital who are deaf."

"Well, that's what they're teaching Dre, and he's getting so good at it. I haven't quite learned what I should. I only know some things like bed, book, car, house, and 'I love you.' I love you is my favorite because he knows how to say it back to me, even though he doesn't know what it means. Sometimes I get him to do it back, but then sometimes he doesn't and that's okay by me. I'm getting a little full just talking about it."

May Esther had tears just falling down her face. "Candace, I prayed for you and Dre all the time. But I never imagined the Lord will give him such a gift. I couldn't be happier for anyone if I tried. Those times I dreamt about, how I wanted to be, how I wanted life to be for me and you….You would always tell me 'Maybe it's not too late, May'. I hung onto those words. You never really talked the whole time. You just sat back and listened to me ramble about my hopes."

"That's because I thought life was just me and this big house, and a baby who didn't talk. But listening to you talking about dreams, school, and traveling around the world gave me hope. We gave each other hope. Ms. Agnes would walk around this big old house and praise God, singing Baptist hymns. She always liked 'The Lord Will Make a Way Somehow.' I never asked what that meant, because I was a child. She'd ask me if I prayed, and I would say 'yes ma'am, when I go to sleep.' I believe Ms. Agnes prayed for me more than I prayed for myself."

"I'm sure she did. When I'm in church, Candace, that is the safest place for me. God is everywhere, and no matter where I am, He's there too. I didn't know that growing up, and I had to go through life with Nicky to realize God was there watching over me the whole time. Even in my bad decisions. He has been there for both of us. Look at how well Dre is doing. The prayers from Ms. Agnes were also for your life without her in it."

"I haven't been to church much you know, with Dre not liking the noise. Since things have been better, maybe I could start back. All I really need to do is give him a book or a string, and he might sit there long enough until Pastor Lee start yelling. This felt just like old times, laughin, talking like two hens."

"I do have something that I want to share with you." I was so nervous I could barely wait to tell May.

"Okay, what is it? Do you want me to guess? Are you going to tell me?"

"Well, they wanted me to talk to these professors from up North about Dre's fits and him not talking. Ms. Ferby, the blind teacher, wanted to meet one of those gentlemen, who works with kids like Dre. May, you know I was so scared. But then I finally agreed. Mr. Anderson came here from New York a few months ago."

I don't think May Esther blinked once. She sat back and said, "Candace, spit it out."

"May, you are worse than Dre when he wants jelly cake! So, Mr. Anderson started working with Dre at school with different things. He has also come up to the house and worked with him. Dre loves him. He responds well and he's so calm when he is around." I hesitated, not sure if I should say what I really feel, but it was May Esther. I knew I could tell her anything.

"Well…I think we are courtin'." May was in shock and put her head down. "May, are you okay? What's wrong?" I ask in concern.

She reached for her tissues from her pocketbook, and cried. May was crying and I was crying, and I don't know why. I asked her, "Oh, May, are you okay?"

"Sit down, Candace."

"I thought you would be happy and surprised."

She sat across from me in the white rocking chair on the side of the house. I hadn't sat on this side of the house since Ms. Agnes died. This is where she and Miss Pearl would sit and have long talks. I was a little girl then, running around eating dirt and making mud pies from the water spilled over from the big well. "I'm okay, Candace. I'm sorry, but you don't know how happy I am for you. I prayed so many days for you and Dre. I wanted a better life for both of us. God is something else. Candace, I had nowhere to go and He allowed me to live across the way from you. There were so many times I wanted to give up, but Jesus sent me to you. You always had kind words for me. You listened to me and talked to me when everybody in knew what Nicky had me doing."

"I wanted the best for you too, May, but I just didn't know how to help you, when I couldn't even help myself. We were both a mess with a little bit of hope we held on to."

"Okay, now that we're done crying, I'm listening." May was so comfortable in that chair drinking her Coke and nab.

"I had no idea meeting Mr. Anderson would turn into long walks, long talks, dinner, and Dre falling asleep in his arms. It all happened so fast. While on our way home from the diner in town, he grabbed my hand and grabbed Dre's hand on the other side. It just felt so right. He lives in New York, but he took a liking to the south, so he spends most of the time here in Jacksonville working with Ms. Ferby."

"Candace, this sounds like a love story."

"May, hush your mouth. I reckon…I like him, I just hope and pray mama and papa does too."

"Do you love him, Candace?"

"Remember when you told me I how would know? Well, I reckon I do."

"Has he said it to you?"

"No, no."

I felt so embarrassed talking about this, but I couldn't help but smile. I can finally tell May.

"But I can't wait. I love how he loves playin' with Dre, even though Dre doesn't show affection, but Dre will run to him if he hears a loud noise. Oh no! I realized it was time to pick up Dre from the schoolhouse. "May Esther, I have been running my mouth and forgot my baby. Walk with me, May. You can unpack later.

"Sure, Candace, I'd like that. The walk will do me good. It's something I rarely got to do around here when I was with Nicky. Folks around may not remember me."

"I reckon not. You are a nurse and all now."

"Ms. Ferby, I want you to meet my dear friend May Esther."

Ms. Ferby turned around slowly, put her walking stick to the side, and reached out for May Esther's hand. May couldn't stop staring at her with a surprised look on her face. "It's a pleasure to meet you, ma'am." Ms. Ferby fixed her glasses on her face as she moves from side to side. "Did Candace tell you about Dre's learning ability? I am so proud of all his achievements thus far. Ms. May Esther, your friend is a wonderful mother. She was frightened as any mother would be, but she didn't give up on us when she didn't understand. I am so proud of her too."

"Yes, ma'am, I can see all the Good Lord has done for them both. You are heaven sent, Ms. Ferby."

I'd never imagined anyone saying they are proud of me.

"I don't see Dre Ms. Ferby, is he out back with the other chillun?" I asked.

"Mr. Anderson said he would take him since you were a little late."

I got stuck in my shoes; I could not talk or move with fear all over me.

"It was a pleasure to meet you, Ms. Ferby. God bless you. You are a gift from God." May said, stepping in to talk for me when she saw my face of fear and no movement. "Ms. Candace, I hope that was okay—that I allowed Dre to go with him."

I almost swallowed my tongue. "Yes, ma'am, Dre seems to take to him so well."

"Yes, I am so happy to hear that. I knew Mr. Anderson would make a difference. You know, he told me he is thinking about moving here to Jacksonville. He loves this southern living."

That let me know that Ms. Ferby didn't know that he has been keeping company with me. "Thank you, Ms. Ferby; we better hurry home."

I was running up the road, sweating so much. I forgot I had May with me. "Candace, stop please! I'm running in my Sunday shoes." We were both laughing. I then stopped so May could catch up with me. What was happening to Dre right now with Thomas? I didn't even know if Thomas knew how to really handle Dre alone. All these questions were running in my mind. Father, God, please take care of my baby.

"Look, Candace, look at me." I was so sad and scared. I fell right into May's arms. "I'm so scared, May," I told her.

"I know, but Dre is safe. You have been around this man enough to know he would do no harm to you or Dre. I've learned by going to church that I have to pray instead of worrying."

I listened to May; I always have. She somehow knew how to calm me down when I'm scared. "Let's just keep walking; we almost to the house."

"Okay." I grabbed the tail of my dress and wiped my eyes. I looked up, and I could see Thomas and Dre way up the road. "Look a there…see, I told you," May said. "I knew things would be alright. Candace, sometimes you must stop right where you stand and pray. Now don't go fussing him out. Just be calm and act happy to see them."

Lord knows I wanted to slap Thomas for taking my baby.

The closer we walked up the road, the better I could see Thomas showing Dre how to throw rocks in the pond under the bridge.

"I can't believe how big Dre got. He is growing up like a beanstalk," said May. Thomas looked our way and tapped Dre on the shoulder to show him we were standing there. Dre was excited about throwing the rocks, so he didn't care who was standing there. I was excited for him. He would pick up the rock, look at it, feel it, and after Thomas said, "Let it go, Dre," he threw it in the water as hard as he could. He'd watch the water splash in the air when the rock hit the water and clapped his hands together. Dre hardly ever showed emotions…well, not happy emotions. Thomas wiped his hands off and walked over to us.

"Well, hello. I hope you didn't mind that I brought Dre home, Candace. He walked up to me at school and took my hand, so I said, 'I guess that means "Take me home."' We made a few stops along the way. I remember throwing rocks in the river as a young boy when visiting my grandmother in Mississippi," said Thomas and laughed with a hardy laugh. May laughed with him to ease my mood and I just smiled. "No, I thank you. I was a bit worried, but I knew you two were okay. I'm glad he felt comfortable being with you."

May winked at me as if I'd done well. "Oh, this is my best friend May Esther I told you all about. I got so caught up watching Dre I didn't introduce you two."

"It's nice to finally meet you, Ms. May Esther. I heard so much about you." He reached out his hand to shake May Esther's hand.

"I have heard so much about you too, Thomas." Watching the two of them meet and talk about Dre touched my heart so. I had two people in my life, along with mama and papa who made me feel like I mattered, and they cared about me and my boy. I had the Lord to thank for that. "Well, we better head on home. I need to get supper started."

"Okay, I think these rocks will have our attention a little while longer." He laughed again, the laughter deep and bubblin' up from his chest. Even though Dre didn't smile too much or even know what it means to smile, I felt in my heart he was happy.

May said, "I just want to take Dre in my arms and kiss his sweet face. He is as cute as a button."

"Hey, Dre."

Dre looked up at May and Thomas signed to him to say, "Hi." Thomas lifted his fingers to show Dre, and Dre fixed his fingers to sign "HEY" and went back to picking up more rocks. May was in shock.

"I can't believe my eyes. This is not the same Dre I knew last time I was here."

"He is changing every day."

We started on to the house and neither one of us said nothing. You could hear the soles of our shoes kicking the dirt and rocks. "I can't believe I spent time in that house locked up. A prisoner in my own house." We got close to May and Nicky's old house, and all the bad memories came back to May's mind. It's boarded up now. I reckon that was a good feeling for her.

"Well, to God be the glory. He had other plans for me."

"Yes, He did, May."

May and I hold hands, walking like we two happy children.

"Candace, I'd been holding my breath long enough, but Thomas is a pretty man. He is sturdy, like he could move a truck. I am so happy for you. I love how he looks at you. His eyes were shining.... He loves you, Candace. God sent this man here to love you and Dre."

"You ever felt happy but afraid to be happy, and think you don't deserve to feel that way?" I said. "I walk through this big house and picture Ms. Agnes sitting at the table smiling. It feels like her spirit is here. Remember we used to talk about dreams, May? I never dreamt this for me.... I could not imagine if you told me that someone was going to care for me and Dre. I hoped for this feeling. The sadness is now gone."

May wipes her makeup after crying again. "We going to have a pot full of salty tears if we don't get supper started."

CHAPTER 29

Thomas

I already missed May Esther. I didn't know when I'd see her again. Before she left, she told me to be open to love because I deserved it and that it's a gift from God. She was so happy. I could see it in the way she acted and talked. She spoke of the Lord the whole time she was home. She read the Bible to me and marked some things I should read in Ms. Agnes' big family Bible. I don't think I'd opened it since she passed on. Ms. Agnes said the Holy Bible is life's map, and if you follow it, you won't be lost.

I enjoyed laughing and talking with May Esther so much. Dre warmed up to her as if he remembered her. She read to him too, just like she did when she lived next door. Dre would not let May Esther hold the books though. He had to give them to her. We all laughed at that. He used to have a fit when I touched them, but he just stops what he is doing and takes it from me. May's soft voice soothed him, I believe. Some nights when May was here, she and Thomas looked on as Dre would look at the words in the ABC book and signs. Nobody but Thomas knew if what he what saying was right. I thank the Good Lord that May got a chance to see how good Dre was doing. She saw that God answered her prayers for us too.

Thomas reminds me all the time that chillun like Dre have funny ways about them. They repeat the same things over again. Dre touched his chair at least thousand times before he sat down. I'd been seeing this behavior with Dre since he was about three or four. I told Thomas papa would get him small racing cars and that he would line them up one after the other. He would take his time making sure they were straight. Papa would say, "No, son, slide it across the floor, make it go fast." papa tried to grab one to show him, and Dre threw a fit, snatched the car, and lined it back up until it was almost perfect.

"You know, it seems like his brain doesn't want to be disturbed," Thomas said. "I've been in meetings where the doctors don't know what to call what Dre has, but the teachers won't give up learning how to work with them."

"Is that why Ms. Ferby wanted you to come here, just for Dre?"

"Yes, that was the plan." Then, Thomas walked over to the bookcase, stared at the books, and turned and looked at me. I felt so shy the way he looked at me. "That was the plan: to come here to the south, and study the behavior of the children who have those peculiar behaviors.... But I never thought I would like it here the way I do. I said I would be here for maybe a month, and go back to New York."

"Maybe you like it here 'cause of the good cooking in the south. It cannot be the weather you complain about all the time.

You always say it's too hot. You might not be that hot if you stop wearing that suit and hot tie every day," I said.

He laughed so hard, he had to hold gut. His loud laugh scared Dre, so he ran out of room, into the kitchen, and hit head with his fists over and over again. He threw his book across the kitchen floor and covered his ears. Thomas walked over to him, and says, "Dre…Dre…it's okay; take my hand."

Dre had his eyes closed and scooted until he felt Thomas' shoes. Thomas was so calm, as he always is. He lifted Dre to his feet and Dre started hitting his ears. I was afraid for him.

"Do you think his ears hurt?" I asked Thomas.

"It's the noise that bothers him. Especially unexpected noises." Thomas sat on the chair, and Dre sat on the floor between Thomas' legs. Dre was rocking back and forth with big tears in his eyes. I leaned over to see if he would let me look at his head. He'd hit his head really hard. I looked at Thomas, as if I wanted permission. My baby, if only he would only let me kiss his head. As I held back my tears, I got on one knee and slightly rubbed his head to see if he'd hurt it. Thomas never moved the whole time I was checking on Dre. Dre got up, picked up the book, and ran to his room upstairs. I looked at Thomas and he smiled. "What's so funny, Thomas? I am a wreck. It's been a while since he had a fit."

"Well, I wouldn't call it a fit." Thomas said. "The noise startled him." He paused and then said, "For some children, the calmer things are in their surroundings, the better they feel. The constant humming that he does is another way of him soothing himself. Every day, Candace, we will hope for the best."

CHAPTER 30

Preparation

Thomas knew how to make the things I worry about seem like nothing. I don't know what I would do without him. He helps out around the house. He keeps the grass cut and cooks us some fancy city meals. Dre learned new words and read new books Thomas received from up north. Thomas was now cutting Dre's hair. He put small cotton pieces in his ears so the scissor and razor noise won't scare him. Papa used to have a time cutting Dre's hair. I would feed him jelly cakes the whole time to get through it.

I was going to see mama today. I had to be ready for all them questions. I already know the first one: "You think he gonna marry you?" I hadn't let Thomas stay the night. He was not that type of man. I wouldn't dare let him stay over until we were married. If I did, I'm sure Ms. Agnes would come down from Heaven herself and preach to me.

"Mama, you home? Papa you here?"

"I'm outside, Shug."

"Hey, mama. I thought I would smell some of your blueberry's and biscuits walking up the road." mama wiped her hands and face on her apron and hugs me so tight as she always does. Lately, when I see her, she looked very tired in her face. Mama was working just as hard as papa around the house and farm. They got out there before day and left to go help pick tobacco.

"Mama, you feel okay?"

"I reckon I got a little pain in my hip that bothers me. You know how it acts up when it rains."

"You been at the farm this morning?"

"I walked there with papa to bring some of them collards and field peas in for supper. Your papa still out there."

"Mama, on those hot days, please be careful. You and papa can get a heat stroke out there. You know some days you don't feel good enough to get out of bed."

Mama laughed at me saying that. "You sound just like Ms. Agnes. You have an old soul from taking care of her so long. The Good Lord is taking care of me and your papa. You and Dre too. Mr. Anderson still come to your house, and does Dre still take to him?"

"I can tell that Dre feel something special for him, and he trusts him. I am learning new things about Dre too, mama."

"Well, what about you? How you feel about him?" mama got this big grin on her face; *Oh no*, I thought. "Candace, it's been a long time since you been courtin'. I want you to know when a man is liking you. You been so busy with Dre, you stop thinking about yourself. You sure he ain't no fast-talking city man? If he still around, he is looking for something."

I really didn't know what to say or where to start first with her.

"Mama, I like him but I'm scared."

"What you afraid of, Shug?"

"I don't know. I think I shouldn't be somebody he would like." I wanted to cry on mama's lap. "I love Thomas, I reckon. Well, I know I do, and my baby does too. Dre's daddy made me feel something I never felt before and left me. He doesn't even know he got a baby in the world."

"The Good Lord doesn't make no mistakes I know you already know that. He knows why things happened this way. You were a gift to me and your papa, and Dre is a gift to you. It wasn't so easy for me, Candace, but I made the best of it. Ms. Agnes changed my life—well, our lives. I was out there picking cotton at sixteen and living at home. Ms. Agnes brought me in to help her. She took care of me and helped me take care of you. After I had you, Ms. Agnes was the only person I could trust, and she never treated me like I was her slave."

Mama stood over by the stove looking up at the grease stains on the ceiling. "I felt right shamed when Ms. Agnes left you her big house. I worked day and night cooking and cleaning in that house, and she left it to you. I never wanted you to see my moods about it. Deep in my heart, I knew Ms. Agnes was worried about your life with me. That ole biddie." mama laughed, and then quickly turned that into tears. "Mm, mm, mm, Shug. I didn't mean to cry in front of you."

"It's okay, mama."

"Look here, Candace; listen, baby. It is okay to love him back. He loves y'all. From what you say about him, sound like he wants to make you happy. Open your heart because it's never been open the right way. The Good Lord wants us to be happy. He brought that man from the north to love you. The Lord works in mysterious ways, somethings we ain't gonna understand, but by and by, we will. You know we don't question the Lord. When you say your prayers tonight, thank The Lord for everything and Thomas."

It'd been a while since I been up to the schoolhouse. Thomas had been picking Dre up and bringing him home. Dre loves it. I can tell. He knows the exact time to go to the door and sits right there on the floor looking out for Thomas through the torn piece of the screen at the bottom of the door. As soon as he sees him, he grabs his bag and runs out the screen to him. I didn't know what to feel some days, jealous or happy. There were some evenings when I was sure Thomas wanted to stay. It was late when he left some nights. He had to walk to Cagey's store where he rented a room over the store. I'clare I get scared for him walking on that dark road late at night, but he never makes a fuss.

"Good morning, Candace." He kissed me on my cheek. Every time he does, it feels like the first time. He is here for Dre a little early this morning. I haven't wakened Dre yet. "You slept well? You look bright eyed and bushy tailed. I know I'm early, but I wanted to sneak a kiss in this morning before I get on the road with the Busy Bee." Thomas laughed that deep chest laugh. I love hearing it so much.

"You know it will be alright if you don't feel like carryin' Dre to school. I'm up doing a little bit of everything anyway." Thomas shook his head and said, "How about this: you get dressed and walk with us this morning? I think he would like that."

I never thought to say, "Let's take him together." "Well, okay, it will take a few minutes to get Dre up and dressed as well as myself," I said.

"Great! Send him down when he gets dressed and I will keep him busy matching crayons."

It was a beautiful October morning. Thomas and Dre were walking ahead of me, swinging their arms. It was clear that he didn't look like Dre. I don't care what people say. Like May Esther used to tell me: "You may not be ready for change, but you just have to accept it as a change for the better."

Thomas looked back at me and winked. He slowed up a bit so he could help Dre tie his shoes. I knew this was going to take a while. Dre must play with the strings like they are toys over and over again, and Thomas just laughed at him. "I think after we drop him off at school, maybe you and I can spend the day together and enjoy the beautiful weather. I thought maybe we can go into town and eat lunch and go to the beach. Have you ever been to the beach before, Candace?"

"It's been a while." I answer without hesitation.

"Well then, that's the plan. We'll hop on the bus and go to Topsail beach. I asked a few people about the beach since I was planning on making the South my home. I love the freedom here. Well, not so much freedom, but it's easy living. I love everything about this little old town."

Thomas was staring at the sky, with the biggest grin and the prettiest white teeth, as he took Dre into the schoolhouse. His words were smooth, and the people made fun of the way he talked 'cause he was from New York.

I walked into school and Dre sat in the corner, away from the other kids. He had everything he needed in that corner. He loved it. Thomas added new pictures each week for him to finger spell. Ms. Ferby was sitting in the back of the class, waiting for the other teacher to settle the children down. Dre is rocking back and forth looking up at the finger spelling board. Dre got fidgety and walked to the black board and scraped the chalk across the board. The sound from chalk on the board surprised the children, and Ms Ferby, and they made so much noise its scared Dre. He ran and hid under his desk. I was afraid he would tear the room apart, as he's done in the past. The noise got Ms. Ferby up on her feet. She heard the chatter from the children, and she knew Dre was afraid, while Thomas and the other teacher tried to calm the class down. Ms. Ferby made way to Dre, moving slowly between the desks. "Dre, it's okay." Ms. Ferby had the softest voice, and sounded like she was singing. "Dre, it's over now; no more noise." Thomas was right there to help Dre back into the chair at his desk. The children were so quiet you could hear a pin drop. I reckon they were used to it. The sweet little deaf girl, Sarah, never stopped playing with her ball she always held in her hand. She never heard a sound. I whispered to Ms. Ferby, "Thank you, how you and your help look after Dre." She stood up and reached out to give me a handshake. "We are so pleased with Dre. And I don't know what we would do without the help of Mr. Anderson. You know he comes to me some days and touches my hand. I think when he does that, he wants me to teach to him.

"He has a special gift of learning finger spelling. It is a blessing to have him learn how to communicate without speaking."

"I lay awake at night and think about all that is happening in my life, Ms. Ferby," I said. "I didn't think Dre would have this chance."

"I have the gift The Lord gave me that I don't have to be like everybody else to be normal. I don't believe children belong in a mental hospital when they blind, deaf, or can't speak. My mama made sure that would not happen to me either, Ms. Candace. I imagined she felt the same way you did. The Lord sends out His angels in human form." I hugged her for being our angel.

Chapter 31

The Beach and My Heart

"The water feels so warm on my feet. What makes a city man like you like the beach?" I asked Thomas.

"My father used to take me and my mother to a place called Coney Island. It's a huge beach in New York City. It wasn't the cleanest, but it was the best. I was about Dre's age. I love the memories of my childhood. We didn't have a lot. We were poor just like the people in my neighborhood, but I had the best time." Thomas rolled up his pants legs and tucked his tie in his back pocket. He bent down, made a house out of the sand, and a sign with his fingers sliding through the sand.

"What does that sign mean?" I kind of laughed when I said it. It was a funny looking symbol. "The house in the sand is your house, and the other symbol means 'I love you.'"

Oh my, oh my. I had that feeling in my stomach. I was so nervous and scared, I felt like needed to use the bathroom. He kept staring at me, as I almost tore up my sweater pulling on it.

"I didn't make you bashful, did I?" He stood up and pulled me up from the sand, still looking at me. I turned away because I knew I felt the same, but I was scared to death. I couldn't help but look back at him when he held me.

"Candace, I never thought it would turn out for me this way. I came here on a mission: to teach a little boy with limited abilities, and go back to New York. Ms. Ferby told me she needed me for about two months. A few months turned into a few seasons. I know you are scared of what you are feeling, and I don't blame you. But I know what I feel for you is true. I have grown so fond of Dre, and I think about you all throughout the day. When I lay down at night, and first thing in the morning. I love working at the school. I think of all the ways I want to help Dre. I want to help Dre with all there is to learn."

I hear every word he is saying, but I am still stuck on "I love you." I cannot believe he loves me. Mama was right. He loves us both. "I've been doing all the talking, Candace. Do you have anything to say?"

I really was at a loss for words. "First, can we please sit back down on the quilt?"

"Sure, we can. Are you alright?"

"Yes, yes I am fine. Just a little surprised, I reckon."

"Candace, you don't have to say it back. I wanted you to know how I felt. It's important for you to know how I feel."

"I can say I feel the same way, Thomas. I'm scared, but I feel that I have love for you too."

He grabbed my arms, and we rolled on to the sand. We both laughed the happiest laugh.

"So, what do we do now?" I asked Thomas.

"We don't have to do anything you don't want to do. But I would love to keep courting you until we get ready for marriage," he said.

Marriage! This is all a dream. It has to be. I felt so excited all over again. I knew it showed. I couldn't stop smiling. Me married? A husband? Dre will have a father? I couldn't believe this was happening to me. What could I have done to deserve this joy I feel? My life was sounding like one of them books May Esther reads about love.

I knew Thomas saw how I felt, and it sure ain't sadness. "I frightened you again with the thought of being married?"

"Yeah, a little. I haven't imagined myself being with anyone who wanted to marry me. It's always been me and Dre. Ms. Agnes knew this before she passed. She told me: 'One day, someone is going to come into your life and sweep you off your feet and you will get married and have babies.' I held on to every word and didn't understand it, but for it to happen this way is something else."

"Honey, sometimes, life doesn't happen the way you planned it. Then you realize later that God has something better for you. Far better than you can imagine. I came here to teach and change a child's life, but I fell in love with his mother, and you both changed my life. I would like for Dre to be the son I never had. I know it's not right to question God, so I am thankful for this assignment. You and Dre changed my life for the better. I plan on changing yours for the better too."

My Prayer
Dear Lord, hear my prayer.

I didn't think I mattered to anyone. I know I will always matter to You. I wake up in the morning and see daylight, and I know I matter to You. You watch over me and Dre. My life now is nothing I could have imagined. Thomas says he loves me. No one ever told me that beside mama, papa, and Ms. Agnes.

I think about all the good that has come to me, and I can't believe it. I wanna thank you, Lord. I remember the bible verses Ms. Agnes had me say 'til I knew them in my heart. She had hope and faith and wanted me to have it too, even in the bad times. Her words are so clear in my mind, "Hope. All other ground is sinking sand, Candace. You won't sink if you have hope. The Lord is your hope."

Please watch over me and Dre with Thomas. I ask, Lord, that you let Dre speak words, and you show me and Thomas how to protect him. I love you and your son Jesus.

In Jesus' name I pray.
Amen.

Chapter 32

I let Thomas sleep on the couch last night 'cause of the bad storm. I didn't feel right making him walk up that dark road. Dre didn't like the rain or the thunder. Thomas put cotton in Dre's ears to shut the noise out. He sat next to Thomas on the couch, with his favorite ABC book in one hand and the yo-yo Thomas bought him in the other and fell asleep.

"I don't know how you gonna sleep with Dre stretched out like that."

"It's okay," he laughed. "I can sit up and sleep. I have fallen asleep like this many nights when I'm too tired to go to bed. Can you kindly put the pillow under my head so I can lay back?" I fluffed up my softest pillow and placed it behind him. "Thank you. You can go up and go to bed, dear; we will be fine. If he wakes up, I will walk him up to his room."

"No, I think I will sit with y'all for a while."

"Are you a little uneasy about dinner with your folks Sunday?"

"Yeah, with all the questions mama gonna ask you. She may ask about your mama's kin folk. I start laughing. Mama already got us married in her head. I told her to be easy on you. I ain't worried about papa at all. He will tell mama to be easy too. My papa is a kind, soft-talking man who loves the Lord."

"It's fine with me if she wants to ask questions. They only want to make sure you're in good hands. It will be fine."

I stared at Thomas when he was not looking. I took in his thick eyebrows, thin lips and real nice dark skin, and his thick mustache. He was slowly falling asleep sitting here. Much as he does at the schoolhouse and taking time with me and Dre, I'm sure he's worn out.

Thomas was a genius to me. He knew so much about everything. He made a letter chart for me here at the house to learn the finger spelling symbols like Dre. Dre was surprising me everyday. He was starting to use a spoon to eat his food. When he wanted more to drink, he pulled on my dress instead of throwing it across the room. Thomas said he didn't know if Dre will ever be able to ever speak. They were still doing research on his ways. I could hear mama in my head: "The Lord don't make mistakes."

"Thank you, Thomas, for showing me what it feels like to be cared for. You even shown me ways to love Dre, even when he doesn't know what it means to be loved."

"Candace, I love you. I care for you and I love you. You don't have to thank me anymore. I haven't felt this way for anyone. You are a strong, beautiful woman."

"Strong and beautiful…I don't know about that. I'm as weak as a leaf falling off a tree."

"It takes a strong woman to handle a child with peculiar behavior, fits, outbursts, and no speech. You never gave up on him.

Even if it meant you had to hide him to protect him. I see strength in you. You manage this big house and turned it into a home, a safe place. The Lord put obstacles in your life to walk you through them. Hold your head up and be proud of yourself for once." I couldn't stop smiling. Those words sounded so good to me, and to think he was talking about me!

Thomas went to see about a teaching job at Georgetown High School. He would still teach Dre and help Ms. Ferby. I reckoned I'd stop by and check on Ms. Pearl—see if she needed a little help getting around the house. She never had chillun, so I helped when I could. I knew Ms. Agnes would've wanted me to.

"Ms. Pearl, ma'am, its Candace."

"I'm in the parlor, Candace." Ms. Pearl's house smelled like medicine. She sucked on that snuff all day long. She didn't make quilts like she used to. She and Ms. Agnes would sit in the parlor and make the most beautiful quilts you'd ever seen. They taught mama, and now mama and a few ladies from the church house sit around after supper on Sundays and make quilts. They sell them to the White people in town. "Ms. Pearl, did you eat today?"

"No; I reckon I'll wait for lunch."

"It's past lunch, ma'am. You have to eat, Ms. Pearl, or you gonna pass out in here. I will prepare supper for you and clean up a bit."

"I thank you, Shug. You always been a good girl," Ms. Pearl said looking at me as I moved about the house. "Look at you, Candace. Hair so full and thick. Your mama still press it?"

"No, ma'am. I go to the new shop I town."

"It's right pretty. I've heard so much good things about my boy Dre. Ms. Ferby tells me he is coming along pretty good."

"Yes, ma'am; I am right proud of him. He makes words with his fingers. I even know a little myself. I'm learning right along with him."

"You know, if they can do all they did with Hellen Keller, you know Ms. Ferby can work wonders. The Good Lord has blessed her so. Ms. Ferby told me that Mr. Anderson is sweet on you. Is that right, Candace?"

I knew that was coming sooner or later. She was still nosey as can be. "Yes, he is very kind to me and Dre. He is very smart too."

"Y'all been courtin' some time now I reckon? Candace, you a pretty young woman. You should be courtin'," she said and smacked on that snuff like it was fried chicken. Every other word, she had to spit in that old metal green bean can. I felt sorry for her. She never married, and she wasn't always as nice as she is now. I guess that's why nobody paid her no mind.

"I like him a lot, Ms. Pearl."

"Has he met your folks yet?"

I laughed a little. "No, ma'am, we goin' up there Sunday after church for supper."

"Lord, I 'spect your mama gonna be one happy lady. We got to give you a nice wedding. You should let your Aunt Lucy make one of them tall coconut cakes."

"Ms. Pearl, shame on you. That man did not ask me to marry him."

"Well, what you taking him to your mama's for? He wants to ask them if he can marry you. That's why. He is a smart man, and knows he has to do it this way."

I walked out of the parlor and started supper.

What if he planned to ask me? *Oh goodness*, I thought. *Maybe I should ask him if that what he plans to. Maybe not.* I walked back into the parlor and found Ms. Pearl fast asleep. Too much excitement, I guess. All that talk about a wedding. "Ms. Pearl, can I ask you something?"

"Oh, I'm so sorry, Candace. I drift off and on all day. Was I snoring?" That tickled her so she had to spit in that can again. "No, ma'am. Ms. Pearl, you think I should ask Thomas if he plans to ask mama and papa?"

"Would you say no if he did ask to marry you?"

"I reckon I would say yes."

"Then let the chips fall where they may. Let the Good Lord do His work. I need to get me a dress for the wedding." Ms. Pearl looked back and started laughing again. "Candace, I reckon Sis. Agnes is shouting from heaven."

Chapter 33

Supper at mama's

The leaves from that big oak tree were just about gone. Sitting on the porch before the day starts made me think about how Dre had grown. If someone was to tell me my life would turn out this way, I would have not believed it. He got so now he minds me. I can tell him to put his books back and he does it. It may take him a while, but he does it.

Every evening, I heat up the water in the wash basin and give him a bath and watch him play with his army men and race cars papa gave him. I have to stay on schedule with him every day, like Thomas tells me. It makes a big difference. It is funny that with all the changes that had been happening in our lives lately, I hadn't put him off track. I knew what he liked and what he didn't like.

Dre loves Thomas, and it shows. The previous day, he'd grabbed Thomas's hand and walked him to the porch to sit on the steps. Thomas taught him something new just about every day. You just have to teach them what you can, so can they be understood.

I knew mama wasn't gonna understand all this talk today. I 'clare, I was so scared about supper with her and Thomas meeting today. I was praying that mama and papa would like him. I need to get up from here and get ready.

"Mama! We're here," I called out as we entered mama's house. Dre walked to the wood stove and sat down with his book and army men. "Have a seat, Thomas. They may be on the back porch."

Mama walked in with her hair pinned up in a bun. She looked so pretty with it up instead of pulled back. "Hey, Shug, dinner is ready. I was helpin' your papa light the trash out back."

Mama was nervous. She kept wiping her hands and moving things around. I smiled at her 'cause it was funny to me to watch her act like that. I guess it came from working as a maid all her life.

"Candace, that's the only thing you could find to put on today?"

"Mama, I'm alright. Thomas likes this dress."

"Then I reckon it's okay. You didn't bring Dre?" She was so used to Dre running through the house.

"Yes, ma'am. He is in there with Thomas by the fire."

"Hush your mouth; Lord have mercy. Candace, the Lord is so good."

"Yes, ma'am; Dre has changed a lot. Thomas says he is brilliant. As soon as you teach him something, he learns it right away." Then, mama leaned in and whispered in my ear so Thomas couldn't hear her, "You think he will talk, Shug?"

Mama had been asking that question since he started school. I was used to her asking that question, but it still bothered me. That's all she thought about, when I hardly ever thought about Dre not talking. "I don't know, mama; only God above knows. But if he doesn't, I am learning to understand what he wants and feels by the way Thomas teaches him."

"I know you told me about all that stuff. I am just goin' keep on praying. One day, The Lord will allow Dre to say something. I don't know if I will learn all that finger mess."

"It's finger spelling, mama." We both laughed to change the mood. "Let's eat, Shug," she said.

Papa and Thomas sat on the back porch after supper. After all the questions mama asked Thomas at supper, I knew papa felt shamed. Thomas was very polite and patient with mama. I was the one rolling my eyes at her. Thomas talked about the research and everything they were doing with Dre and other children all over. Then mama interrupted him and said, "Do you think they can get him to talk, say something?"

I sat there, sippin' sweet tea and staring at mama through the glass. "Well, you know Ms. Robena, we haven't quite figured that out yet."

But mama couldn't stop. Then she said, "So he ain't retarded?" papa walked in and said, "No, that boy ain't retarded! He got plenty sense. I went outside and he done stacked all them little pieces of wood one by one. I watched him the whole time as I smoked my pipe. They were perfect. At times, he would stop and swing his arms back and forth, almost like he was thinking." papa just laughed and changed the mood.

"No, ma'am; we don't consider Dre retarded."

But papa knew how to stop mama from going too far with her mouth. "Bean, that ain't nothing you ask Thomas." papa and folks called mama 'Bean', short for Robena. Papa looked at me 'cause he knew I was upset. I was upset but trying not to show it. "I will go get Dre and give him some cookies. I'll be back." Dre met me at the screen door with a cute little smirk on his face. When he looks like that, all I could think of was his love and that The Lord was whispering something good to him.

"Dre, you want some cookies?"

He swings the door open and sits down on Thomas' feet. I see mama couldn't take her eyes off of them. Dre eats the cookie fast and tries to snatch another one, but Thomas makes a sign with his hands to wait. Dre tapped on his leg a few times and I gave him another cookie. Then he ran back in the house with it. Thomas said, "Say 'thank you,' Dre." Dre took his hand and put the open palm of his hand over his mouth, and then pulled it away. The sign is similar to blowing a kiss. I remembered that sign, but I don't ask him to say it as I should.

Dre went to the wood stove and played with the keychain Thomas made for him. Mama couldn't believe what she saw Dre do, and papa lookin' on with a proud smile on his face. "Well, I'll be, maybe he is changing. What about them fits, he don't have 'em no more?" Thomas sat back so I can answer, but mama was lookin' to Thomas for the answer.

"No, mama, he been calm most days."

"Ma'am, I hope you don't mind me saying this, but there are a lot of things that may change over time as research continues,"

Thomas put in. "Unfortunately, there are things that may stay the same throughout his life. There are doctors and scientists tracking all kinds of behaviorist problems. With my help, Ms. Ferby, and Candace, Dre will live a normal life, as much as possible."

Mama said, "Don't forget The Lord's help."

Thomas looked at mama with assurance and says, "Yes, ma'am. With the Good Lord's help."

I helped mama clean up after supper. "Thomas, you had enough?"

"Yes, ma'am. Thank you kindly. That was a fine meal." I'd never seen mama smile so much. She felt at ease with Thomas telling her about Dre and his future. They liked him. Papa got up and walked out to the back porch. "Thomas, I reckon you need a break from all that meddling Bean was doin'. Let's head out back for a spell." Thomas smiled at me as mama watched, and he followed papa out back. He called Dre out with them.

Mama and I finished cleaning up. She couldn't wait to get out there to see what they were talking about.

We walked out back, and they were sitting out there under the big oak tree. That was where papa and my uncles sat under after Sunday service. Mama and I sat on the chairs on the porch. "Mama, you like him?" I was afraid to ask but I did.

"Shug, I didn't know what to think when you told me about him, but after today I love him."

"Mama!" We both laughed.

"You know what I mean, girl. It seems right, Candace. He loves you and Dre. I can see it."

"Mama, I love him and we told each other. We were at the beach, and he said he loves me, and I said it back. It's almost like a dream. I used to wake up and not remember my dreams for years, ever since Ms. Agnes passed. But I remember my dreams now. They about me and Thomas."

"Baby, I want you to be happy. You don't know how I worry about you and Dre. You a young mother like I was when I had you, but I had Ms. Agnes and my mama. All that you have gone through raising Dre, and all the attention and care he needs. You one of the best mothers I know. Even better than me."

We hugged. It always felt good to hear mama say how she felt about me. I loved to hear it.

Papa and Thomas sat out there and laughed so much. Papa even showed him how to chop wood. Papa teased him about being a city boy. Dre was stacking the wood while he chopped. I looked back and mama started on her quilt, looking happy and humming her favorite church hymn, Great is Thy Faithfulness.

"Thomas, we better head on back before dark," I said to Thomas. He looked wore out after all that chopping. He ain't used to all that hard work with his hands. "Sure thing, honey," he said, and I had butterflies in my stomach when he said that.

I hurried back in the house before mama could say something. I know she was praying and thanking God at that moment. As soon as we got our things together to leave, Thomas called me out to that back porch where they were sitting. Papa and mama were sitting next to each other, and Thomas was standing front of the doorway. "What's wrong?" I asked him. Mama had a handkerchief in her hand as if she had been crying. I didn't know what to think. I knew Dre was okay as he was sitting on Thomas' feet playing.

"Well, I want you to sit here for a few minutes." His voice was shaking, and his arms were swinging back and forth. I looked over at mama and she began crying and smile. I felt a little relieved.

"Candace, I've been in North Carolina for some time now, and I guess you can say I found a new life. A life that no one would have imagined I could have. I am settled here now, and I want to settle here with you and my boy here. I talked with your parents and asked them to have their blessings to marry you."

Good Lord, what is happening? I thought. The porch was spinning and I began crying. "Both of your parents said yes. Now I want to ask you if you'd marry me, and let me love and protect you and Dre," he said.

Papa stood and moved to the side so Thomas could kneel on one knee. He never told Dre to move off his other foot, and Dre didn't move either. Thomas reached in his pocket and pulled out the prettiest ring I ever saw and put it on my finger.

"So, will you marry me, Candace?"

"Yes, Thomas, I will marry you; yes, Dre and I will marry you!"

He stood up, grabbed me from the chair, kissed and hugged me. I was crying, mama was crying and papa, for the first time I've ever seen, was crying.

My life was not how I planned it. I wondered if Ms. Agnes or mama prayed for this. Maybe I prayed it and didn't realize it would come true. Maybe I really did have hope all this time.

Chapter 34

~

"*I Do*"

Yesterday was one of the happiest days of my life. The first was Dre's birth. When Thomas asked me to marry him, I thought about how I had never even been to a wedding before. I didn't really know how to do it. When I told May Esther, she said, "You won't have to do it by yourself. Your mama and I will help with everything. I will be there this week, Candace." May was full when I told her. I heard on the phone whispering "Thank You, Jesus. Thank You, Jesus."

It took mama, Aunt Ella, Aunt Maddie, Ms. Marie, and Ms Mamie and a few of the women in the church a whole week to prepare the food. Papa, Uncle Doug, Uncle Johnny, and Mr. Atlas and the men from the church house set up the chairs and tables to eat on. As soon as May got home, she decorated the church so prettily. She put green pinecones on each table, and she picked flowers from mama's flower patch. She had my grandmother's favorite crape myrtles sitting in small clear glasses shaped like pears that Ms. Agnes had stored in the attic. She put white ribbons that she brought with her from Georgia and placed them on the back of each chair and around the alter where the Pastor stood. Ms. Ferby had the children from Dre's school make red hearts, and May stuck them on the wall as you passed by when walking into the church house. Aunt Lucy made her famous three-layer coconut cake with white icing as my wedding cake. She put holly on it with green leaves and small red balls. The top of the cake had prayer hands that May also brought with her too. I 'clare she'd thought of everything. All this fuss made just for me.

Well, the day was finally here. I walked in the church, with papa holding my arm as tightly as he could. Mama had Ms. Nezzy make my dress. It was a full white gown with lace around the neck, waist, and arms. She made the tail of the dress long, so it could drag behind me as I walked. My hair was curled up with pieces of holly pinned in it. Each curl was perfect. Oh, my goodness, I couldn't believe how many people were there for my wedding day. Everyone was smiling, eyes were wide open with surprised looks, and some stood to make sure they could see every piece of the ceremony. Mama was looking up in the church ceiling rocking from side to side, wiping her tears thanking the Good Lord. Ms. Pearl and Ms. Ferby were sitting in the same row of chairs as mama. May Esther stood in the back to guide the trail of my dress as it followed me and papa.

It was time to walk down the aisle.

Waiting at the end of the aisle was the prettiest man I'd ever seen…Thomas. I now knew what that meant. He had on a black suit with a white shirt and a black bow tie papa had given him. He shaved the hair off his face. It made him look younger.

Dre was sitting on the floor next to Thomas. He was playing with something Thomas gave him to keep him still.

Thomas and I had talked about whether Dre should come to wedding the night before, and if it would be too much for him. Thomas said, "He should be there; he is our son. We want people to see that his life can and will be normal. I will put the cotton in his ears to distract him from the noise."

Thomas and Ms. Ferby thought it was a good idea use the cotton a few months ago, and it continues to help. Dre was still for the whole ceremony.

I was glad Pastor Allen didn't talk too long. Before I knew it, he said to Thomas "You may kiss your bride now." We turned to each other and when I looked into his eyes. I 'clare I saw pieces of my life in them.

In his eyes, I saw me and Ms. Agnes sitting in the parlor room when I was a little girl, telling me how God will protect me. I saw Dre's birth and how Aunt Annie said, "It's a big healthy boy!" I kissed Thomas and fell into to his arms, and he held me. I felt a tear fall from his eye, but I didn't look at him. I didn't want him to let go. The church clapped and praised the Lord. When the organ music started playing, I felt Dre wrap his arms around both of Thomas' legs. In that moment, I knew God was breathing into me. Dre kept holding on even after we kissed. Everyone laughed. Thomas looked down at Dre to make sure the cotton was secure before we walked out together as man, wife, and son.

It was time for May Esther to go back. She had to go back to her nursing job in Georgia. The night before she left we made a promise that we will keep in touch and remain friends for ever. May was happier for me than I was for myself. "Candace, the wedding was beautiful. I know the Lord was pleased."

"May, can I tell you something?"

She stopped packing and sat down on the bed. "Yes, Honey you can tell me anything."

"I'm scared, May. I haven't said this to anyone, not mama or Thomas. It's the same feeling I had when Dre was born. I was so afraid not knowing how to be a mother, now I am afraid of not knowing how to be a good wife. Did I say yes to Thomas out of fear?"

May smiled and said, "Honey, you have nothing to worry about. That man you married knows all about you and Dre, and he knows this is where he wants to be. I don't believe he thought twice about marrying you. He has worked with Dre for over a year and look at Dre now. He loves Dre as his own. None of us thought Dre would be where he is now. He is doing things only the Lord could make happen. You are living a miracle from The Good Lord. You are going to see more miracles too. Thomas is a smart man, and he knows what he wants. This a dream-come-true for you. Remember we used to say hope was all we had? You said Ms. Agnes used to shout, "On Christ the solid rock I stand; all other ground is sinking sand."

May was right. The Lord had been our hope through everything we have been through. The tears were falling from May's eyes. I reckoned she was thinking about how far the Lord brought her too.

"Guess we and can both say hope: All other ground is sinking sand, huh? It was the only thing that kept us from sinking. I'm thinking about all those times with me fighting to leave Nicky, and you being scared people would find out about Dre could not talk, and take him away from you. Two colored girls from the south who shared dreams with each other and prayed to God for one another."

May was the strongest woman I knew next to mama and Ms. Agnes. She was right; we were watching our lives change right before our eyes.

"I wish you could be here all the time." We hugged each other. The hug meant we were proud of each other. "You will be fine. The Good Lord ain't done with you yet if we stand on that solid rock—Jesus. I will be back soon. You are a married woman now, so enjoy this way of living and loving, my sweet little sister."

"Candace, please hurry before the sun goes down." That was Thomas rushing me for our day trip to the beach. Dre loved the water so much. He got so that he lets the water come to his legs before he runs back to the sand. He did that about a hundred times. We didn't care, 'cause it made him smile. Thomas said it was time to make a sandcastle. Dre watched every move Thomas made and began to do everything Thomas did. Dre wasn't satisfied until his was perfect. It was a beautiful day.

We've been married for six months now, and waking up each morning never felt so good. Thomas was asked to work at Georgetown High School up in Richlands as a counselor. Most days after Dre goes to school, I look after Ms. Pearl, and cook and clean for her. Thomas has done so much work around the house. The grass is so pretty in the yard. He painted the bricks along the walkway white. Papa and Uncle Doug helped Thomas build a play area in the house like the one he has in his classroom.

Mama loves the house. She never came over much before. Now that Thomas fixed it up, she says it looks more like my own home instead of Ms. Agnes'. He got Dre's bedroom looking like a school. Papa sanded down an old table and made it into as a desk for Dre. He got letters and numbers all over the wall in different symbols. The teachers at the school made them for him. He took off the front of the dresser drawers and made a bookcase. Thomas is always bringing home a book so Dre can carry it to his room and put it on his shelf.

Everything is happening so fast. Dre is becoming more aware of things. He is more settled than he has ever been. Ms. Ferby says it all the time. He listens to me and Thomas when we he tell him to stop doing something he shouldn't do. He just walks away as if it doesn't bother him. It is so hard to believe where he was, and where he is now. Thomas has to still go to New York sometimes to work with the professors there. He told me they may have settled for a name for Dre's peculiar behavior—it will be made known to the public soon. It is all so complicated when Thomas tries to explain it all to me. Thomas says it is as if they live inside in their head, and not concerned with the world outside. His brain functions different. When I am looking at him playing and hummin' to himself, I daydream about him saying to me, "Look, mama." I am okay if he never does it. My hope is one day he will. That is a prayer only me and the Lord knows about.

"How was your day, honey?" Thomas was able to buy an old car from Mr. Gus. He takes so much pride in it. Dre loves it too. Once Thomas gets him to school, he doesn't want to get out. He loves to look out the windows, rollin' the windows up and down and touching all the knobs. Thomas has to give him a piece of candy every morning to get him out of the car. Ms. Ferby and the teachers tease Thomas for giving him sugar for breakfast.

Dre still sits in a corner in the class. He knows how to put the cotton in his own ears now. It doesn't bother him as much, but I think he feels better with them in his ears. "My day was busy. It's different dealing with older children with behavior problems. It's hard to get through to them, and they get frustrated a lot faster than the younger children."

"Will Dre go to a school like that when he gets older?"

"Well, hopefully there will be other great opportunities for him. The scientists and doctors will not give up on this situation. This affects both colored and White children. Some doctors may think it needs to be treated with medicine. Others are involved in the program in New York, working with the children hands on, to see what they are capable of learning without medicine. Ms. Ferby has always believed that any child can be taught—whether they be blind, mute, etc."

"I am so thankful that they haven't had to give Dre any medicine. I was worried when he was havin' them fits of spitting, and fighting, running off. But The Lord didn't see fit."

"No way, honey. Dre responds to teaching, learning, and with the safe environment we have provided for him, that will never happen. At this point in research, medicine has not been an option. Possibly early on before they knew what it was, I am sure they wanted to. I meant to tell you the other day I was in the bathroom shaving, and I didn't know what Dre was looking for. He looked through my bag that I had on the floor. I noticed he was frustrated. I stopped shaving and sat on the floor next to him. I had the shave cream still on my face. I had my handkerchief in the side pocket of my pants. Dre snatched the handkerchief and tried to put it in his ears. He took the tissue and tried to put it in his other ear. I realized what was happening. He could hear me scrape the hair from my face and the noise from the razor bothered him. He didn't see the cotton. He knew that if he had something to cover his ears, the noise wouldn't bother him. That boy amazes me every day, Candace."

"Lord have mercy, Thomas. Maybe that's what he looking for when he runs around the when we are talking and laughin' too loud."

"You might be right, honey. This shows how much he pays attention, and how sharp his memory is. I will put the cotton ball symbol on his sign board. The more we work with him, the better he'll be able to show us what he needs here at home too."

Over the past year, we have figured out that the loud noise takes him into a fit. I thought people would think we were foolish when they see the cotton in his ears. But if it helps my baby, I'll do it. Now I don't have to ever be ashamed about what The Lord blessed with me.

Ms. Ferby told Thomas she was coming over to the house today to talk to us. Thomas didn't seem too worried about it. I often think about Ms. Ferby. A blind teacher walking around, smarter than most people that can see. She always says she is guided by the Lord. Mama says that means she got the faith of a mustard seed. This is what the Lord wants us to do: walk by faith and not by sight. I understand more and more about faith and hope. Thomas loves the Lord and he always is telling me to believe in my prayers when I pray. To believe that The Lord will answer them.

There was a time when I didn't know what it meant to have hope. Mama, May Esther, and Ms. Agnes would tell me to have hope. Ms. Agnes told me time and time again, "When you stand on hope, all other ground is sinking sand. She said stay out of God's way. He don't need no help. The Lord put all these people in my path because He knew me and Dre would need them.

When Dre was a baby, I would rock him to sleep and I would kiss his fat cheeks and pray over him and all the things I wanted for his life. At that time, I had no idea he couldn't talk. I didn't know this would be his life, but God did. Now I know everything is alright.

Chapter 35

With God, All Things Are Possible

"Ms. Ferby, it's so good to see you. I hardly get to see you since you back and forth to Georgetown High school."

"Thank you, Ms. Candace. I have been busy. I love it though. I will keep teaching as long as they want to learn. Technology has improved for blind persons. I am learning as I teach as well."

"Did I beat Thomas and Dre home?"

"Yes, ma'am, Thomas takes him around town before he gets home. They are like two kids in that car." We laughed. Ms. Ferby likes to sit by the door wherever she is, even at the schoolhouse. She looks like her face is glowing. "Ms. Ferby, you look so pretty." She just smiles and laughs a little. "Thank you, Ms. Candace. Since I cut my hair, everyone sees my face now."

"You still look like a young girl."

"Ms. Candace, you filled with compliments today. You making me blush."

"Thomas mentioned you wanted to talk to us. Do you want to wait until Thomas comes home?"

"No, I can talk to you. I wanted to talk to you about Dre's progress. Progress means how Dre has been doing the past year." I don't know what she is going to say, but it can't be all bad. "You know, I remember when you first brought Dre to the schoolhouse. I wasn't there. I was out of town. My teachers told me you were scared, and they weren't sure if you would even leave him. When I got back and spoke with you at the schoolhouse, I could sense the fear. You talked slow and unsure. I wasn't sure what you were thinking, but your mama had already told me you were afraid someone would take Dre away from you if they knew he couldn't talk. I told her that I believed with all my heart that school was the best place for him. Sometimes, you got to look past your fears and feelings in order to see what the Lord has for you. We had some good times with Dre, and some pretty bad ones, but me or my teachers never gave up. I trusted in the Lord. I pray for all my students. I pray for me and the teachers, that we get what we need to help each child. I am just a blind woman who loves to teach. I felt you trusted me the day you brought him to school."

I sho' do remember those good and bad times. When I picked him up from school and asked how he is doing, she would always tell me, "We all have good and bad days. We understand that it's hard for Dre to express himself, but he will be alright."

"Ms. Ferby, I will never know how to thank you."

"I don't know how to thank you for trusting me with your son."

I started crying like a newborn baby. She made her way over to me feeling for things that could be in her way, and wrapped her arms around me. It was the cry I needed, but this time it was happy tears, if there is such a thing.

"Aww, let it out, honey. You are a wonderful mother, and I am sure a fine wife to Mr. Anderson. Are you okay, Ms. Candace?"

"Yes, ma'am, I was so used to crying because of sadness, and now, all I cry is happy tears." I dried my eyes and looked up at Ms. Ferby. She was crying a little herself. "You can sit back down, Ms. Ferby, I'm okay now. Thank you so much for being the blessing that I never thought I deserved."

"The blessing is having the opportunity to have Dre as one of my students. I always pray that I make a difference in my students' lives. I know you hoped for someone to show you how to take care of your son. Hope is that little part of faith that pleases God until He shows up and answers our prayers." I looked out the front screen door, and see Thomas and Dre driving up. My heart is full as I watch them get out of the car. "Sounds like they're home."

"Yes, ma'am, they are home. I was thinking to myself while looking at Dre, Thomas, you, I thought of Ms. Agnes, and what she would say so often."

"What's that, Ms. Candace?"

"She would look up to the sky and say, 'Hope: All other is ground is sinking sand. Yes, Thank you, God, for hope. Thank the Good Lord for hope."

The End